Murder Is Developmental

(A Susan Wiles Schoolhouse Mystery)

by

Diane Weiner

Copyright 2015 by Diane Weiner

For information, email **Cozy Cat Press**, cozycatpress@aol.com or visit our website at: www.cozycatpress.com

COZY CAT
PRESS

ISBN: 978-1-939816-78-8

Printed in the United States of America

Cover design by Paula Ellenberger
http://www.paulaellenberger.com/

1 2 3 4 5 6 7 8 9 10

\

This book is dedicated to all the loving and hardworking preschool teachers and daycare workers everywhere.

Chapter 1

Lynette pulled off the highway and onto the country road leading to Westbrook Developmental Preschool. Pine trees flanked the road and the morning sun poured through the windshield. The few houses they passed were set back from the street, all with long dirt driveways punctuated by traditional mailboxes. Lynette brought her toddler to the school every day before work, but this morning, she had an additional passenger—her mom.

"Mom, should I pick you up when you're done volunteering at the preschool?"

"No, Lynette. Dad's gonna get me. My car's in for an alignment." Susan fanned herself with the newspaper she'd brought along. "Is the air working in this car? I'm beyond hot flashes, so I know it's not me."

"It's working. A record-breaking, scorching New York July is all. The beat officers are lobbying for these new-fangled summer weight uniforms. Thank God we detectives can wear street clothes." Lynette wore a sleeveless, cotton blouse with a peasant skirt and espadrilles. Her blond hair was pulled into a ponytail.

"Ha! Audrey thought she'd be escaping the heat when she comes for a visit next week. I bet it's hotter here than in Florida right now." Susan hesitated, "I hope she'll still come."

"If being in her upper seventies doesn't stop Audrey from traveling, neither will a heat spell. Nothing's going to keep your mother away from her new-found family. From what I've seen, she's every bit as stubborn as you are." Lynette's baby daughter, Annalise, fussed from her car seat.

Susan said, "Why the heck did Audrey tuck that newspaper clipping into my paperback when I left Florida? I can't stop thinking about it. What did she mean *help him*? She wrote those words right across the clipping…in black marker."

"I think it was cruel—no, cowardly—to ask for your help like that, Mom. And then to refuse to tell you anything over the phone…"

"She says it's complicated and she needs to explain in person. It seems out of character for her to be so cryptic. When we were in Florida, she was nothing but direct and to the point. This doesn't feel like her." Susan sighed, "I'll just have to wait a little longer."

"Mom, since when are you so patient? I know it's killing you. You've been checking it out already haven't you?"

"Believe me, I tried. Too bad the Westbrook Police Department doesn't own some of that facial recognition software. If you did, then we could at least find out the man's name."

"Better yet, we'll run it through that machine that reads DNA from photographs."

Susan's jaw dropped. "What? You have that?"

"Of course not. I'm just yanking your chain, Mom. If a machine like that existed, you'd have seen it on *Law and Order* by now."

Lynette continued up the winding two-lane mountain road, which became a gravel driveway as she approached the octagonal-shaped school. The walls were made of glass, which optimized natural light and enhanced brain development. Susan pulled the car visor down and checked her appearance in the mirror. She brushed her honey blond hair, and made a mental note to schedule a root touch-up and a bang trim. From the backseat, Susan heard Annalise say *school*.

"See, Lynette! This place is teaching her advanced language skills. She's not even two yet and she can say *school*."

"You heard *school*? I heard *shoe*. She probably kicked off her sandal."

"My granddaughter is brilliant. She looked out the window and saw the school and said *school*. I'm sure of it."

Westbrook Developmental Preschool had been founded at the height of the multiple intelligence hysteria, when every family owned a copy of *The Mozart Effect* and played classical music for their babies in an effort to create math wizards. The school's curriculum included painting class, daily playground time (even in the midst of winter), and music class. Being a retired music teacher, Susan Wiles somewhat bought into the premise, and volunteered to teach music at her granddaughter's school. Westbrook High, where Susan normally volunteered, was on summer break, and—after all—every minute she spent with Annalise was a treasure.

"Mom, can you grab the diaper bag while I get Annalise out?" asked Lynette, as she opened the rear car door and unbuckled her daughter. "By the way, her shoe is on the floor."

At the school entrance, Annalise stomped on a colorful welcome mat, while Lynette pushed open the heavy glass door. The school smelled as if Clorox wipes had recently attacked the toys and equipment. The two women stepped into an indoor lobby/ playground, complete with a table and water play station. The classrooms radiated out from the center, the office being the first door on the right. The director,

Vanessa Harrison, a Halle Berry look-alike in her mid-forties, greeted them.

"Susan, we just got in a new shipment of rhythm instruments. Aren't you excited?"

During a recent sleuthing adventure, Susan had experienced how deadly a particular percussion instrument could be. Not wanting to squelch the director's enthusiasm, she merely smiled and replied, "Great, Vanessa! Can't wait to give them to the kids."

"Ahhhhh!" An ear-piercing scream filled the school. A young brunette teacher with a stylish bob flew out of the teacher's lounge. "Look, look!" She was out of breath, and jumping in place.

The director clasped the young teacher's wrists. The jumping subsided and was now merely mild bouncing. "What is it, Katie? Are you okay?" she asked.

"It's...it's..." The young teacher fanned a stack of money at them. "Money! These are hundred dollar bills. Tons of them!"

"Katie, did you win the lottery?" said Vanessa.

"No. I stopped for doughnuts this morning and I was looking for that big platter we used for the holiday party so I could put them out for everyone."

A pudgy, middle-aged woman with a soft face and a wide smile ran into the lobby. Noticing the money and the general uproar, she grabbed Katie's arm and spoke in a high-pitched voice. "And there was a wad of money in with the doughnuts?" She was obviously the older of the teachers. Her wild, curly hair ran down the back of her tie-dyed t-shirt.

"No, of course not, Rachel," replied Katie. "That's ridiculous. I reached way up in the cabinet." She mimed the motions. "Then I pulled out a stack of dishes and a silver serving ladle. I thought the platter was behind them, but instead I felt this stack of paper. When I got it down and looked, it was a bundle of money!" She kissed the green stack.

"How did it get there?" asked Rachel. She whispered, "Are you going to keep it?"

"I thought about it, but no. I have to turn it in to the police," replied Katie.

"And how long has it been there? No one goes in that cupboard. I stored the platter and serving spoon up there myself after the holiday party," said director Vanessa.

"So it hasn't been there too long," said Katie, still wide-eyed over her discovery.

Susan tapped her index finger against her cheekbone. "Must have been put there within the last six months."

Lynette pulled out a legal pad and jotted down notes. "Katie, can you come by the police station after school and sign a report? I'll take the money to work and write up the paperwork. When I get to the station, I'll check and see if there have been any recent robberies or reports of lost money."

Sighing, Katie said, "For a brief moment, I thought I was rich."

"If it was lost or stolen, maybe there's a reward attached," said Lynette. Katie's blue eyes sparkled. Lynette turned to Susan.

"Mom, call if you wind up needing a ride home." Lynette bent down and gave Annalise a kiss goodbye.

"Well, ladies, I'm afraid it's back to work," said Vanessa. Parents started bringing in their children, and the director put her finger to her lips as if to say, "Don't talk about this in front of the parents." At that moment, the third teacher on staff, Shelley Hall, came through the front door holding a bag of Meow Mix.

"Shelley, you can't keep feeding those strays. You promised months ago you'd either find them homes, or drop them off at the shelter," said the director.

"I can't help it, Vanessa. I can't bring myself to put them in the shelter, and I already have half a dozen of my own at home." Shelley, a petite brunette with hazel eyes, was in her thirties. Susan knew that she lived alone with her cats and never mentioned an ex-husband or boyfriend. She and her colleague, Katie Mitchell, sometimes socialized outside of work. Rachel Steinberg, married with grown children, was a mother figure to them both.

The director shook her head at her three employees and one volunteer and went back into her office. Susan, Katie, and Rachel headed towards their classrooms. The school custodian, as wide as he was tall, approached Shelley and filled her in on the found money.

"Do they know who put it there?" whispered Shelley. Her eyes scanned the lobby.

"Not so far," said the custodian. "Let's keep it that way." He narrowed his eyes as he spoke. Shelley nodded, took a deep breath and slipped into her classroom to start the day.

Chapter 2

Susan's husband, Mike, picked her up at noon. It was his lunch hour, so they stopped at Vinny's before dealing with Susan's Prius. Vinny's was Westbrook's iconic Italian pizzeria. The tables were covered in red and white checkered table cloths and the walls were decorated with Italian landscapes. The aroma of freshly baked pizza greeted customers at the door.

"We had some excitement at the school today," said Susan. She filled her husband in on the hidden money as she chomped on a crusty piece of garlic bread.

"She should have kept her mouth shut, stashed the money in a tote bag, and taken off for Aruba," said Mike, swishing his hands together.

"Just like you would have done," said Susan, smiling. Mike was the most honest man she'd ever met and she knew he'd never do such a thing. He was a few years Susan's junior, and in spite of discussing retirement ever since Susan had left her teaching position a few years back, he still worked in the permits department at City Hall.

"So, Jessica Fletcher, how do you think the money got there?"

"There are three teachers, a director, and a full-time custodian on staff. If any of them had that kind of money, they wouldn't still be working at the preschool."

"What about parents or volunteers, like you?"

"It was in the teacher's lounge. I can't imagine a parent going in there and stashing money in the cupboard without being noticed. And why would someone leave money at the school?"

"I don't remember hearing of any robberies. In this town, that much stolen money would have definitely made the news."

"Lynette took the money to the station and she's going to look into it."

"I see that twinkle in your eye," said Mike. "The scent of a fresh new mystery. You won't be able to resist getting involved."

"Well, at least it's not a murder this time. Not likely to be danger involved here."

"If there is, will it stop you? You always jump in without thinking about me or Lynette. You make us crazy with worry and don't even care."

"You know I care. I've matured now that I turned 63. I'll look before I leap, Girl Scout's honor." Susan raised three fingers. She glanced at Mike's plate. "Mike, why aren't you eating your pizza?"

"I'm not hungry. I'm feeling a little off."

"You must be off. I've never known you to leave a half-eaten slice of pizza on your plate. Especially not Vinny's pizza."

"You want it?"

"Of course I do." She reached for the pizza.

"Let's go pick up your car. I've got to get back to work."

Later that day, when Susan got home, Johann and Ludwig, her precious cats, nuzzled against her legs. She changed into a t-shirt and baggy shorts, then relaxed on the sofa with the remote and a can of Diet Dr. Pepper. Just as Connie Chung was about to reveal the one summer item Justin Bieber couldn't live without, her cellphone rang. It was her birth mother calling from Florida.

"Audrey, you're still coming in next week, right?"

"Wouldn't miss it for the world. Just called to give you the flight information. By the way, will my grandson be there? I miss him."

Susan still cringed when Audrey referred to Evan as her grandson. Susan's Mom was Evan's Grandma and just because she was no longer alive, it didn't give her biological mother Audrey permission to step in and take her place. Especially since she had only come into their lives a few months ago.

"Like I told you before, he's doing research at Columbia this summer." Susan felt her own chest puff out whenever she talked about her son, the med student. "It's almost a two-hour ride from here, so he's staying in the city, but we see him whenever we can." Susan had won the battle over where Evan would be spending his summer. Evan was a medical student at Washington University in St. Louis. It was bad enough that he was so far away all year, but Audrey had tried to get him to spend his summer down in Florida with her!

"Can't wait to see everyone," added Audrey.

"Audrey, can't you tell me anything about that cryptic article you stuck inside my book? Who's the man in the picture?"

"Like I already said, I'll tell you when I get there. It's just too hard to talk about over the phone. I'll see you soon."

Susan released her frustration with a primal grunt. Patience had never been one of her strongpoints. Cleaning the house generally helped her stop obsessing. She threw in a load of wash and ran the vacuum. Before she knew it, Mike would be home. She debated cutting up some chicken and fresh veggies for a stir-fry on the one hand, and making a meatloaf with instant mashed potatoes on the other. Meatloaf won. Maybe she'd open a jar of brown gravy to pour over it. As she was taking the chopped meat out of the fridge, she heard a knock. Lynette came in with Annalise.

"Lynette, I didn't expect you. Is everything alright?" She took Annalise from Lynette and smothered her with noisy kisses.

"Everything's fine. I thought I'd stop by and let you know that Jackson and I searched through police records and found no reports of stolen or lost money. We checked for prints on the cash she found, but only found Katie's."

"So you want me to keep my ears open?"

"Sure, Mom. You do that. By the way, I have some happy news. Jackson and Theresa are expecting a baby."

Susan squealed. "Really? That's wonderful. Theresa will be a great mom. That partner of yours though…not sure he's mature enough to handle being a father."

"Mom, Jackson is a sweetheart and super reliable. He'll be just fine. Speaking of sweethearts, my own hubby will be getting home soon, so I'm going to run."

"Relay my congrats to Jackson for me. I'm going to call Theresa myself." Lynette's partner's wife, Theresa, had taught fourth grade at Westbrook Elementary, the school where Susan had taught music before retiring. Almost as an afterthought, she added, "You know, Lynette, Annalise could use a sibling. She'd be a great big sister."

"Mom, don't start that again. She's not even two yet. Besides, how can you be so insensitive? You know how hard it was for me to get pregnant with Annalise. I'm not ready to go through that again."

"I'm sorry, Lynette. You're right. It's just that the thought of another grandbaby…."

"Bye, Mom." In a throwback to her teenage years, Lynette marked her exit by slamming the door hard as she left.

Chapter 3

The next morning, Susan turned up the radio and sang along to Miley Cyrus's *Wrecking Ball* as she cruised to school behind the wheel of her blue Prius. The alignment had done wonders. Still humming, she walked into the teacher's lounge and saw Shelley, Annalise's teacher, organizing a basket full of cellphones.

"Can't decide which one to use?" said Susan.

Shelley laughed. "No, these are the phones I collected for the battered woman's shelter. I'm just boxing them up so I can drop them off after work."

Katie came into the lounge and stuck her lunch in the fridge.

"Maybe today you'll find jewelry hidden behind the creamer," said Susan.

Katie shuffled some of the items around in the fridge. "Nope, no such luck."

"Good morning, ladies. I brought you a treat. These petit-fours are left over from the Junior League meeting I had at my house last night." An auburn-haired woman wearing a Chanel suit came in and set down a tray. *Westbrook has a Junior League?* Susan thought. It was news to her. She got a whiff of expensive perfume as the woman walked past her. Susan recognized her as a parent, but if she'd ever known her name, she didn't remember it.

"Thanks, Marin," said Shelley.

Katie grabbed a pastel-coated petit-four and took a bite. "Delicious, thanks," said Katie.

"You're welcome."

"Hey, I just had a thought. Are you trying to bribe me?" Katie giggled. "You know I don't give grades to three-year-olds." Marin Weatherly's son, Trevor, was in Katie's class.

"Enjoy, ladies!" Marin waved to the director, who was just entering, on her way out.

Susan spent the morning singing through a book of nursery rhymes with each class, holding the pictures up for the kids to see. Then she did her best rendition of *The Itsy Bitsy Spider,* complete with hand motions. Some of the kids were catching on after weeks of repetition and imitated the finger play. She remembered the box of new rhythm instruments, and left the children with a parent volunteer while she went to get them. As she was crossing the lobby play area, she heard arguing. Not yelling. More like a strained, angry whisper. She followed the sound which seemed to come from the large supply closet, where the rhythm instruments were stored. Susan looked around. The lobby area was deserted, so she pressed her ear to the door.

"I know she was here. I followed the GPS. My wife was here last night!" The voice was definitely a man's. She could barely hear the response.

"No, I know nothing about it. I wasn't here last night."

"You're lying and you'll pay for this! Do you know what this is doing to her? To me?"

"Is that a threat? I'll call the police."

"Then you'll be cooking your own goose in the process."

Susan heard heels clicking against the tile and quickly pulled away from the door. She spun around and found herself nose to nose with the director—Vanessa Harrison.

"Susan, do you need something?"

"Um, yes. I came to get those new instruments you said you had."

"They aren't in the supply closet. They're still in my office. Come with me."

Susan followed the director into her office. By the time she'd retrieved the box and walked back to her room, the door to the supply closet was open. Whoever had been in there was gone. It killed her not knowing who they were. It sounded like someone was in danger. Probably one of the teachers. Katie? Shelley? Boyfriend troubles? Maybe it was Rachel's husband, but that seemed less likely.

Susan finished teaching and popped into the lounge where Katie, Shelley, and Rachel were having lunch.

Katie said, "I've about had it with him. We've been dating for over a year and I have yet to meet his friends or his family. Then he storms out of my apartment when I press him about it. He's a first class jerk sometimes."

"The same boyfriend that didn't send you roses at work for your birthday?" said Rachel.

"The same. How did you find your husband, Rachel? I want a man like him."

"I was very lucky. We've been together for almost 30 years now. We were best friends from the get-go. Not that we don't have our moments. Marriage is a lot of give and take."

"And you, Susan?" asked Katie.

"Rachel's right. It's not like every minute is heaven, but I'd rather be spending time with Mike than just about anyone else in the world, although my granddaughter is giving him a run for his money."

"Men!" Katie sighed. "Let's move onto a more pleasant topic." She glanced at Shelley. "Shelley, is that a new Louis Vuitton purse? How'd you afford that?"

Shelley cleared her throat. "Got it on sale."

"Where?" said Katie. "I've never seen them on sale. Even on sale, I doubt I could afford one."

"Sometimes you just have to indulge," said Shelley.

"Speaking of indulging," said Rachel, "any news on that bundle of money?"

"The police have nothing right now. My daughter Lynette said there are no prints, no leads," said Susan.

"I'm hoping for reward money," said Katie. "Hey, maybe then I can by a Louis Vuitton purse like Shelley's."

"Let's keep hoping," said Susan. "I'll see you guys tomorrow."

Susan started sweating the moment she walked out the door. The air smelled like the inside of a steam room. She'd take the ice and snow over this any day. The custodian walked out behind her, carrying a large, clear garbage bag.

"Hey, Eddie. Did someone have a class party? Where'd all that garbage come from?" said Susan.

Eddie jumped as if surprised to be seen. "Well, ugh, kids. Juice boxes, Kleenex…always a mess."

"You have a good day," said Susan. She walked over to her car. *What was in that bag, and why had Eddie been startled when she spoke to him?* She started to drive away and noticed Eddie going back into the school. *What could be the harm?* She turned the car around and pulled up next to the dumpster. The bag was right on top. Holding her breath in anticipation of the stench, she set the bag on the grass and untied it. *What is this?* It was a bag full of shredded papers. She'd never even seen a shredder at the school. Unable to decipher the bits of paper after rifling through them, she retied the bag and threw it back into the dumpster.

Chapter 4

When Susan and Mike arrived at Vinny's for dinner, Lynette, her husband Jason, her partner Jackson Simpson, and his wife, Theresa, were already seated at a table in front of the window. Although it was a weeknight, every table was in use. Susan had spent the afternoon scrubbing the guest bathroom and changing the linens in the guestroom in preparation for her mother Audrey's visit. She now looked forward to a relaxing meal.

"Congratulations, you two," said Susan, hugging Theresa and then Jackson. I'm so excited for you."

"Say goodbye to getting a good night's sleep," said Mike. He gave Jackson a slap on the back. "And start saving those pennies. College is expensive." Susan saw Jackson's brow crinkle.

"Things will be just fine," said Susan. "You can get that baby on a schedule and he or she will be making it through the night in no time."

"And there are scholarships," said Jason. "Where I teach, practically all the students have some sort of scholarship."

"Or there's student loans," added Mike. Theresa put a reassuring arm around her husband.

"I ordered champagne," said Jackson, changing the subject. "And sparkling cider for my better half." He kissed Theresa on the cheek, then turned to Susan. "When's your mother coming? Soon, right?"

"Day after tomorrow," answered Susan. "Still feels weird when I hear her referred to as my mother."

"Weird or not, thanks to her and her medical history, we realized Lynette wasn't going blind. I'm thankful you found her." said Jason. "You remember how awful it was, right?"

"Makes me worry if our baby will have some genetic condition or some problem we don't know about," said Theresa. Her neck and face tensed as she spoke.

"Welcome to the world of motherhood," said Susan. "You'll never stop worrying about your child."

The waitress brought minestrone soup and mozzarella sticks. Susan splashed a bit of sauce on her blouse and excused herself to go dab it with cold water before the stain set. On the way to the restroom, she saw Rachel, the older teacher from the preschool, and her husband sitting at a corner table. She was about to say hello, but neither of the two was smiling. They appeared to be in the middle of a serious discussion, staring at each other, and stiff. They didn't acknowledge her as she walked by.

On the way back from the restroom, Susan noticed that Rachel was crying. Her husband looked as though he was about to shed some tears of his own. *If they were both so upset, why go out to dinner in the first place?* Susan wondered. She took the long way back to her own table to avoid getting too close. She felt as though they needed their privacy.

"Did the stain come out?" said Lynette.

"Yes, mostly. I think I caught it in time."

The waitress brought plates of eggplant parmesan, ziti, and lasagna. Bubbling sauce and baked cheese gave Susan the kind of high she could only imagine addicts got when they took a hit. As they enjoyed their entrees, Jackson's cellphone rang.

"Excuse me. I'll be right back," he said.

Jason turned to Theresa. "When's your due date?"

"March 10. At least according to my calculations. I see the doctor tomorrow."

"I have bags of maternity clothes for you," said Lynette.

"It's great when you can *borrow* maternity clothes instead of buying an entire wardrobe," said Susan.

Lynette glared at her mother. Susan wished she hadn't said that. Now Lynette would be upset with her. Again. She glanced over at Rachel and her husband. Things must have calmed down because at least they were eating. She was truly worried about them. Rachel was so sweet and motherly. The kids and parents at Westbrook loved her. Besides, she was the only one at the preschool who came close to her age.

Jackson returned to the table. "I'm sorry; it was the station. There was a robbery in Glen Oaks. I have to go. Can someone drop Theresa off at home for me?"

"That new development out by the school, right? Before you know it, there'll be no more woods left. Sure, it's no problem. Take care, Daddy," said Mike. Mike flagged down the waitress and asked for the check. Susan did a double take when she looked at Mike's plate and realized he'd hardly eaten anything.

"Is there something wrong with your lasagna?" asked Susan.

"No, I just don't have much of an appetite these days. That's not a bad thing. I still need to get rid of this gut of mine." He patted his stomach. "I'll take it home and bring it for lunch tomorrow."

"I'm pretty exhausted," said Theresa. "I hear you get your energy back after the first trimester."

Susan and Mike drove Theresa to the new house she and Jackson had recently bought. On the way, they passed the preschool. Theresa chatted about how she wanted to send the baby there in a few years since it had a great reputation and was close to home. "Besides, it will give her a head start on getting a scholarship," she added.

"Mike, look!" said Susan. "Why are there cars in the school parking lot? There's never anything going on there at night."

"And there's a light on," said Theresa, pointing. "There, the bottom window around the side!"

"That's the basement," said Susan.

"Maybe they hold AA meetings there or something," offered Mike. "Ask the director about it tomorrow."

I certainly will, thought Susan. *The bundle of money and now a secret night meeting in the school basement?* She felt goose bumps crawling up her arms.

Chapter 5

Susan walked into a yelling match when she entered the preschool the next morning. One of the parents was screaming at Katie.

"I'm going to call the police!" said the father. "Someone opened a credit card using my son's social security number and our address. You're his teacher! You're the only person who has his information and his social. I never give that out. The registration sheet for this school is the only place I've ever written it, other than my tax form."

"The front office has it too," said Katie. Her voice trembled. "Why do you think it was me who did it?" Her face was lobster red. "Maybe your accountant stole it."

The director, Vanessa Harrison, had been outside at parent drop off. When she walked into the school, she immediately stepped between Katie and the parent.

"I'm sure Katie didn't do this," she said. "She's been nothing but reliable. You have no grounds on which to accuse her. If you don't leave right now I'm calling the police to report harassment."

"This isn't the end of this!" huffed the father, pushing through the heavy glass door.

Vanessa spoke calmly to Katie, who was now crying. "His accusation is a bunch of hot air, Katie. Anyone could have gotten ahold of that information. Could've been someone at the pediatrician's office, the accountant's secretary. Don't worry about it; he's just blowing off steam."

Katie wiped her tears. "Thanks, Vanessa." As she walked toward her classroom, one of the stray cats ran in when a parent came through the door. Katie nearly tripped over it.

"What a way to start the day!" mumbled the director, shaking her head as Susan walked up.

"Took a lot of nerve for that parent to accuse Katie like that. He'd better calm down and let the police handle it," said Susan.

"No one is going to treat one of my teachers like that," replied Vanessa. "Poor girl."

"Hey, I wanted to ask you something, Vanessa," continued Susan. "When I passed the school last night I saw cars parked in the parking lot, and the basement light was on. Did I miss something?"

"Really?" said the director. "How strange. No one should be here at night."

"I thought maybe there was some kind of meeting or something. No worries," replied Susan.

"Maybe it's time to get the parking lot security camera repaired. It hasn't worked since I've been here, but it never seemed urgent. We've never had problems with break-ins or vandalism...ever," added Vanessa.

At that moment, Marin Weatherly pushed open the front door with her hip. Susan could hardly see her face behind the armload of art supplies she was carrying.

"Where can I set these down?" said Marin. "They're for making pinwheels."

"Just set them down on the table in the teachers' lounge, Marin," said the director. "Looks like the kids are in for a treat."

Susan grabbed the construction paper off the top of Marin's load. "Here, I'll help you." She walked with Marin.

Inside the teachers' lounge, Katie was sitting at the table, nursing a cup of coffee. She looked up at Susan. "I needed a few minutes to compose myself."

Susan set down the supplies on the table and put her hands on Katie's shoulders. "What a jerk that parent was! He or his wife probably threw one of those credit card offers in the trash and someone found it."

"You should always shred those things," said Marin. "What happened?"

"Nothing," said Katie. "I don't want to talk about it. I have to start class in a few minutes." Her phone vibrated on the table, but Katie made no move toward answering it. "That's all I need, to talk to him right now." She turned off the phone, dumped the rest of her coffee in the sink, and left.

Marin went to set up the project in the lobby, while Susan got ready for her first class. She noticed Shelley and Eddie, the custodian, huddled together outside Shelley's classroom. *Wonder what they're talking about? Surely, she's not telling him to fill up the paper towel dispenser.*

Annalise's class came in for music first. She climbed right up on her grandma's lap. Being related to the music teacher had its perks. Susan opened the nursery rhyme book that she'd borrowed from Shelley and sang the rhymes to the children while showing the pictures. They were clearly too young to sing along, but Susan saw smiles, and gentle rocking as she sang. Certain pages of Shelley's book were dog-eared. Susan figured those were the ones Shelley favored for her own class. She started with *Jack and Jill,* and finished up with *Hickory, Dickory, Dock.*

When the class finished, Susan used her ten-minute break to grab a cup of water from the lounge. Maybe she'd find a bundle of money behind the water cooler! No such luck, but she did see something lodged between the cooler and the fridge. She picked it up, pushing her bifocals back so she could see. She knew exactly what it was. It was an ultrasound picture. Just a blurry, black and white one, not one of those color 3-D shots like Lynette had gotten before Annalise was born. *The date is recent, and the baby is the size of a peanut. Whose is this?* Susan asked herself. Then she slapped her hand to her cheek. *I'll bet this belongs to Katie. Maybe that's why she and her boyfriend are having trouble. Katie is so young. She must be terrified.*

"Hey, what's that?" said Rachel, grabbing a yogurt from the fridge. Susan, deep in thought, hadn't even noticed that she'd come in.

"I just found this." She held up the sonogram image. "Someone around here is pregnant."

"Don't look at me," said Rachel, vibrating her palms in front of Susan's face in a *no way* gesture.

"I think it's Katie's. You know how emotional she's been lately. And fighting with that boyfriend of hers. She wouldn't answer the phone this morning when he tried to call."

"Wow! If so, that's big news."

"Let's not say anything. I'm going to slip this right back where I found it." Susan bent down and stuck the photo back beside the fridge, one hand on her creaking hip.

"Of course not. Katie will share the news when she's ready. She did look a little green in the gills this morning though, come to think of it."

"And how are you doing, Rachel? You've seemed a bit down in the dumps these past few days." Susan decided against admitting to seeing Rachel crying at Vinny's.

"I'll be fine," replied Rachel. "Thanks for asking, though. Remember to get a good night's sleep, Susan. Field trip to the zoo tomorrow. Wear comfortable shoes. Last year I went home with terrible blisters on both feet. You'd think they'd schedule an outdoor field trip during cooler weather."

Susan headed home to finish preparations for Audrey's visit. Her mother's plane was arriving tomorrow evening. Between the most certainly exhausting zoo trip and Audrey's arrival, Susan vowed to get to bed early.

Chapter 6

The sun was already blazing at 9 a.m. when the preschool bus pulled up in front of the zoo. Susan, grasping Annalise's hand, stayed with Shelley's class. Marin Weatherly and a handful of other parents had come along to chaperone. Marin was on the executive board of the zoo and had arranged this special outing. The zoo was unique in that it had an area especially for toddlers and preschoolers. Susan appreciated not having to trek miles through the full zoo in the heat, like she'd done when Lynette and Evan were little.

"Let's see the baby zebra first," said Vanessa. The children—the ones not wandering around like zombies––sat on a miniature set of bleachers, while the zoo representative showed them a handful of zebra food and demonstrated how the baby zebra drank from a bottle. *Even the baby animals smell bad,* thought Susan. The group of toddlers with their short attention spans waddled behind the zoo rep like a line of ducklings. When they reached the monkey cage, Susan plopped down next to Rachel.

"Are you okay, Rachel? You look like you're about to cry."

Rachel's tears flowed. The brood of toddlers stared intently at the comedic monkeys, and Susan discretely handed Rachel a tissue.

"It's money. Again. We're going to lose our house, Susan. We've done all we can to keep it out of foreclosure, but we're about to throw in the towel."

Susan put her arm around Rachel. "I'm so sorry to hear that. Have you talked to a lawyer? Maybe there's still a way out."

"We owe more than the house is worth. If we sell it, we still won't be able to pay off the mortgage. Our credit record will be ruined."

"It's happening to lots of people these days with the housing market like it is. You'll come through it."

The zoo rep led the group to the next attraction—the birds. The children threw seeds every which way. Katie stopped one of her kids from putting a seed up his nose just in the nick of time. Annalise giggled as she threw a handful of seeds, and asked Susan for more.

"We have to get it from the zoo lady," said Susan. She worked her way to the front of the group and retrieved a second handful, winding up shoulder to shoulder with Shelley.

"Poor birds," said Shelley. "Locked in a cage like prisoners at Bayersville State."

Bayersville State Correctional Facility. When I was visiting Audrey in Florida, she got a call from Bayersville State, thought Susan. "That prison isn't far from here, is it?"

"Nah," replied Shelley. "Too close if you ask me. Remember how those two prisoners escaped last year? It took weeks for the police to catch them. Until they were back behind bars, I was scared to go out alone at night."

"Last stop, the petting zoo!" announced Vanessa. Some of the children clung to their teachers, but the majority darted from animal to animal in the small enclosure devoted to young children and young animals. Annalise toddled over to the baby lamb, knocking over a water bowl along the way.

"Remember, teachers and parents!" announced Marin. "The grand opening of the rainforest exhibit is next month. Hope you'll all come back. We're already gotten in a shipment of snakes and amphibians."

"No, Annalise, just pet like this. Gentle. Don't kiss the lamb," said Susan. *I can't take my eyes off her, even for a second.* She pulled a wipe from her purse and cleaned Annalise's lips.

"She sure loves the lamb," said Shelley. "I saw a stuffed lamb in the souvenir shop. Maybe I'll buy it for the classroom."

"That's very thoughtful of you," said Susan. Shelley bent down to pet the lamb, and her keys fell out of her pocket. "Shelley, here are your keys."

"Thanks," said Shelley. They're always falling out of my pocket. Usually I keep them in my purse, but of course, I didn't want to carry it to the zoo."

"Good thinking. The last thing you need is to go home with your Louis Vuitton smelling like animal poop," said Susan. She noticed a charm hanging from the key ring.

"A four-leaf clover? Are you Irish, Shelley?"

"No. It's for good luck. Been on there since I learned to drive, I think."

"Picnic time!" said the director, clapping her hands to get their attention. The group moved to a picnic area beneath a canopy of maple trees. As they were eating, the director told Katie that she'd received a nasty letter from the parent who'd thought Katie had stolen his son's identity.

"I'm freaking out, here, Vanessa. I had nothing to do with that," said Katie.

"I'm just telling you so you don't panic if you get one too. I gave it to the school attorney. He said it's bogus and not to give it a second thought," said Vanessa calmly.

"I can't take any more stress. I broke up with my boyfriend last night. Now this."

Shelley said, "Good for you—about breaking up, I mean. That clown was bad news. You're better off without him, Katie."

"I know," replied Katie, "but I have a feeling it isn't over. He made some threats over the phone, and I got some nasty texts. The man has a temper. I hope he leaves this alone, but I have my doubts."

"If he gives you any trouble, you can talk to Lynette. I know she'll help."

"Thanks, Susan," said the young teacher. "We'll see where things go."

Chapter 7

Butterflies swarmed in Susan's stomach. Audrey would be arriving today and although she'd already spent time with her down in Florida, she felt as if an octopus was squeezing her chest. By getting closer to Audrey, she felt like she was betraying her adoptive Mom. On the other hand, she was angry at her Mom for going to her grave without revealing this secret. She liked Audrey, for the most part, but found her a little too perfect and headstrong—like when she tried to convince her son Evan to work with a doctor down in Florida for the summer rather than coming to New York.

"Come on," said her husband Mike. "If we don't leave now we'll be late. Lots of traffic near Kennedy."

"I'm coming." Susan stopped at the bottom of the stairs and looked around the living room critically. "We never fixed that broken baseboard. Audrey will probably wonder why we're living in a decrepit, old house. Hers was modern and pristine. And her couch had that new furniture smell."

"You're being ridiculous. If she thinks that, she can get on the next flight back to Banyan Beach."

Susan was silent for a few minutes, then asked, "Do you think I've gained weight since I saw her?"

"Susan…stop talking. You look fine."

"She'd better explain that newspaper article."

"She said she would."

Two hours later, they were at the airport gate, waiting for Audrey. Susan spotted her immediately. Tall, brown eyes like Lynette, Hillary Clinton pantsuit.

"Susan! Mike! I can't believe I'm here." Susan gave her mother a hug, sniffing the floral perfume they both favored. She couldn't believe Audrey was 78. With her trim figure and vague wrinkles, she appeared to be least ten years younger.

"Let's grab your bags and I'll take you to our palace," said Mike.

During the ride, Audrey updated Susan on Hemingway High where Susan had subbed as a music teacher when she'd last visited Audrey.

"Schwartz is spending the summer in Austria, working on his book. Gabby the librarian got engaged just before school let out. Manolito, Bibi, and Starr are all at Interlochen up in Michigan. Manolito beat out both Starr and Bibi and is concert master for the summer. Can you imagine how mad the girls must be?" Audrey smiled. It was evident to Susan that Audrey's students were like her own children. At least like Susan's brother, George. The child she kept. *Stop being so catty, Susan. Play nice.* She slapped her own wrist to halt her train of thought.

"Has the drug problem calmed down?" asked Susan.

"So far. Your detective friend Kevin is keeping his eyes on it."

"And George? What's he up to?"

"Same old, same old. No girlfriend in sight. I'm trying to get him on eHarmony, but he won't listen to me."

Dusk was settling in as they pulled into the driveway.

"Lynette and Jason are coming over for dinner with Annalise. Actually, Lynette is making dinner for us."

"I can't wait to see them."

Susan and Mike gave Audrey a tour of the house and got her settled into the guest room. Evan's room still had sports trophies on the bookshelf and video games in the closet. Susan hadn't touched it since he'd left for college. Lynette's old room had been converted into the guestroom after she'd married Jason. They'd replaced the twin bed with a queen and purchased a sleigh bed headboard and matching dresser. Susan bought a pink and green quilt for the bed in anticipation of Annalise sleeping over one day. Just looking at the quilt and thinking of her granddaughter made Susan glow. Johann was curled up on the quilt like a silky, black, ball of yarn. Audrey scratched him behind the ears and Susan heard him purring from across the room.

"Mom, Dad, you up here?" called Lynette from downstairs.

Mike yelled downstairs. "Yes, in your old room. Come on up!"

"Lynette, Annalise, Jason, I'm so excited to see you again!" said Audrey. They exchanged hugs, Annalise clutching Lynette's denim-clad leg.

"How was the flight?" said Jason.

"Fine. I slept most of the way. Starving, though. Back in the day they served meals on planes," said Audrey.

"I'm glad you're hungry. I made a big pan of lasagna," said Lynette.

They followed Susan down the stairs and sat down at the rustic, farmhouse table. It was already set with pottery plates purchased at a local craft fair. Lynette served the lasagna, and Mike retrieved the rolls which had been warming in the oven. Susan waited as long as she could before blurting out, "Okay, Audrey, so who's the man in the picture?"

"He's an old friend. He's been in prison the past twenty years, but he's innocent." She took a forkful of lasagna.

"Innocent of what?" asked Lynette, emphasizing the word *what*.

"He was accused of murdering his wife, but all the evidence was circumstantial," replied Audrey.

Susan asked, "What evidence? What happened?" She leaned forward on the table, eyebrows raised. She couldn't believe how nonchalantly Audrey talked about her friend, the convicted murderer.

"He was out bowling with his buddies. Came home around 10:00 and the garage door was open. So was the door leading into the kitchen. He called out for her, walking through the kitchen into the living room. He found her lying on the floor in a pool of blood, still wearing her jacket. A fireplace poker was on the floor next to her. He immediately checked to see if she was breathing, but she wasn't. He called 911 and held her in his arms while he waited for the ambulance to come."

"Was it a robbery?" asked Jason.

"Her purse was missing, but nothing else. They found no fingerprints on the fireplace poker. The killer must have worn gloves is what they said. None of the neighbors saw or heard anything unusual." Audrey continued eating.

"They had to have a reason to arrest him," said Lynette.

"There were a few bloody footprints heading back out to the garage. My friend says he ran out at one point to make sure the door was open for the EMTs. He had his wife's blood on his sweatshirt, of course. He'd been holding her while he waited for the ambulance."

"And the jury convicted him?" said Lynette.

"Yes, but the blood could be explained, and he had an alibi. His bowling buddies vouched for him."

"I'm not sure what I…" she looked at Lynette, "what *we* can do."

"You're his last hope. Even the Innocence Project turned him down. Susan, you're so perceptive and good at solving puzzles. And Lynette, of course, you're a fabulous detective. Your Mom told me about all the cases you've solved here in Westbrook."

"Where did this happen? In Florida?" asked Jason.

"No, right here in New York state. About an hour from here. Can you believe the coincidence? He's serving his sentence at Bayersville State Correctional Facility. Have you heard of it?"

Susan, memory recently sparked by Shelley's mention of the prison, knew it. A call that Audrey had received when she had visited her down in Florida…that's what the caller ID had said. "Of course, we've heard of it. It's not far from here either," said Susan.

"Will you help me?" Audrey's voice pleaded like a child begging for another cookie. Susan hadn't seen this vulnerable side of Audrey before now. She turned to Lynette.

"Well," said Lynette, "If the police are done investigating and he's already in prison, I'm not sure what help I can be. I'll look it over for you."

"Thanks, Lynette. And your Mom might pick up on something if she looks at it with you." Lynette rolled her eyes. Susan smiled at her.

"Audrey, who is this man?" said Susan.

"He's a dear, old friend. Known him forever. His name is Richard Stirling."

A thought darted like lightening through Susan's brain. *Could it be?*

"Audrey." She took a deep breath. "Is this man my father?"

Audrey's eyes focused on the floor. Susan repeated the question, "Is he or isn't he my father?"

Audrey swallowed her lasagna, stared into her daughter's eyes, and softly answered, "No."

Chapter 8

Even Latin-strength coffee couldn't shake off the restless night Susan had had. Audrey had denied that Richard Stirling was Susan's father, but the tentativeness in her mother's voice had left her unconvinced. Had Audrey concealed his identity because he was a convicted murderer who'd been locked in a jail cell for the past 30 years? The thought made her nauseous. Susan hoped Lynette could get information—examine the case with fresh eyes. After school, she'd do a little internet investigating herself. This time, she was going to work very hard at not stepping on Lynette's toes, or interfering with police business. Meanwhile, she'd call her brother George before he went to work and find out his take on this. She dumped the rest of her coffee in the sink.

"George, it's Susan."

"Hi, Susan. Did Mom arrive in one piece? She couldn't wait to see you and your family again."

"Yes, she's fine. Looks great in fact. I'm calling to see if you know anything about a friend of Audrey's. A Richard Stirling."

George sighed. "Richard Stirling. She's gotten you involved in that too now?"

"What do you mean? She says he was wrongfully convicted. She was pretty convincing."

"Mom has spent way too much time and money consulting defense lawyers, hiring a private investigator, even flying up to New York to see that schmuck in prison. His appeal was denied. Period. She even tried the Innocence Project and they turned down the case."

"She thought Lynette and I could help."

"You can help by convincing her to give up on this. It causes her too much stress. And money. I've got to go to work, but keep me posted, alright?"

"I will. Thanks, George."

Susan drove to the preschool wondering whose perspective was closer to the truth—George's or Audrey's. She rubbed her aching neck muscles with her left hand. Singing with the kiddos would be a welcome distraction today.

When Susan arrived, Trevor's mother, Marin, was changing the bulletin board. Shelley and Katie were sipping expensive coffee drinks. Rachel was sitting on the floor in her gauzy skirt helping Trevor build a bridge out of wooden blocks.

"Susan, did your mother get in safely?" asked Vanessa.

"Yes, she's happy as a clam being here with us. Lynette impressed her with her vegetable lasagna. I'll have to bring her by one day so you can meet her. You two have something in common, Vanessa. She was a principal, too."

"I'd love to meet your mom," said Vanessa. Susan shuddered when the director called Audrey her mom. Birth mother, mother…but not *Mom*. She only had one *Mom* and she missed her every day.

"Time to get to work," said Susan. The children had filtered out of the lobby playground and into their classrooms. Susan entered her own classroom and pulled out rhythm sticks and unbreakable maracas in preparation for the morning. A loud noise coming from the lobby made her jump. She ran out of her room to see what was going on. It was Katie. She clutched her throat and knocked over toys on route to the director's office. Her face was sweaty and red. Shelley, Rachel, Marin, and the director ran into the lobby.

"Call 911!" said Vanessa. Susan immediately punched the numbers into her phone. She looked at Katie. "My God, she's vomiting!"

"What's wrong?" said Shelley, as they gathered around the young teacher.

"Does she have asthma or something? Maybe there's an inhaler in her purse," said Rachel. Marin ran into Katie's classroom to look.

"If she had asthma, I'd know," said the director. "Keep the kids away!" she cried to the other teachers.

Katie dropped to the ground, convulsing.

"Maybe she has epilepsy," suggested Shelley, on her knees at Katie's head. "Should we put a spoon in her mouth so she doesn't swallow her tongue?"

"No! You can't swallow your own tongue. Don't touch her! Anyway, she doesn't have epilepsy," said the director. She ran over to the window. "Where's that ambulance? Come on, hurry!"

"There's no inhaler in her purse!" yelled Marin, returning from the classroom.

Katie's face turned blue. "She's not breathing!" said Susan.

Katie had lost consciousness.

"Where's the ambulance?" cried Shelley. "Wait! Is that it?"

"Finally!" said Vanessa. The doors flew open and EMTs wheeled in a stretcher. They checked her pulse, and started CPR. Within minutes, Katie was loaded into the ambulance and whisked away to the hospital, sirens screaming.

Chapter 9

"Audrey, I'm home!" said Susan. She deposited her Vera Bradley purse on the hall table. Audrey came out of the kitchen, iPad tucked under her arm.

"How was your morning, Susan? I had a great time getting to know Ludwig and Johann. Johann likes to cuddle. Ludwig is more timid, although the string on my reading glasses lured him out from under the bed." Audrey looked away from the cats and turned to Susan. "Are you okay? What's wrong?" Audrey scooped up Ludwig.

"Where do I start? One of the teachers collapsed right in front of us. I'm going to call the hospital in a minute to see what's going on." Susan plopped down on the sofa and kicked off her shoes.

"Collapsed from what?"

"We don't know. The director says she didn't have any health issues. She even went back through her file to make sure. Young girl. When I came in this morning, she seemed perfectly normal, chatting with another teacher, drinking a latte."

"Why don't you call the hospital, and I'll whip up some lunch. I saw eggs and baby spinach in the fridge. How about a frittata?"

"Thanks, Audrey."

"Oh. My God. I just remembered. I think Katie is pregnant. Her poor baby!"

Susan called the hospital, but they wouldn't give her any information. Next, she called the director, who'd followed the ambulance to the hospital.

"Susan," said Vanessa on the phone. "She's still unconscious. Her parents are here. The doctors are trying to figure out what's wrong. They ran a bunch of tests."

"Keep me posted, Vanessa. I'm really worried about her. Her parents must be beside themselves."

"I will."

"And how about the baby?"

"What baby? The doctor didn't mention her being pregnant. I was right there when he spoke to her parents. Surely he would have said something." Susan scratched her head. *If the ultrasound picture didn't belong to Katie, whose was it?* "Should I come over there?" Susan asked the director.

"She's critical, but stable is what the doctor said. I'll call you if anything changes."

Susan took a few deep breaths. *No way will Katie die. Critical but stable. Stable is good. Sitting home worrying won't help, besides, it's not fair to Audrey. She came for a little vacation.*

After finishing lunch, Susan and Audrey explored the quaint shops in the downtown area. Audrey bought George an *I Love NY* t-shirt.

"How charming! It's like a resort town, but rife with businesses the residents use. Not just souvenir shops."

"I come down here all the time," said Susan. "There's a deli at the corner, and every Saturday a green market sets up in the street. Great produce—tomatoes the size of baseballs."

"Look, there's an SAS comfort shoe store," said Audrey. "The cobblestones are hurting my feet through these thin sneakers. Maybe I can pick up something with thicker soles." As they wandered in, the store was empty except for a friendly salesman. He brought Audrey several pairs of sandals and she sat down to try them on.

"Susan, did you give any more thought to looking into Richard's situation?"

"Lynette is contacting the police station he was arrested in to see if she can get any information. I hope they keep files from that long ago."

"I really appreciate this." Audrey tried out the first pair of shoes. "These are comfy. What do you think?"

They're cute. Don't get your hopes up about Richard though, Audrey. What if he really is guilty?"

Audrey's eyes turned fiery. She stamped hard with her thick-soled sandal. "He is *not* guilty. End of story."

Realizing this was a sensitive point, Susan vowed to herself not to bring up the possibility of Richard being guilty again.

"I'll take these," said Audrey.

While the salesman rang up the purchase, Susan changed the subject. She pointed out the window. "See that cute little pastry shop? They have the best cheese Danish. How about a late afternoon treat?"

"I could always eat pastry. I love my sweets."

Another thing I hadn't realized I inherited. Mom rarely ate sweets.

They ordered coffee and Danish, and sat in front of a window framed with frilly white curtains. Susan's phone vibrated.

"Lynette, what's up? Yes, we're having fun, eating pastry at The Sugar Patch."

"She hasn't woken up yet? Foul play? Who would have wanted to..." Susan paused as she remembered Katie's boyfriend and the violent arguments they had. "Lynette, check out her boyfriend. According to Katie, there was trouble in paradise."

"First things first," said Lynette. "Jackson and I are heading to the school to see if there are any clues as to what happened. Most of the kids are picked up by five and it's almost that now. I'll bring Annalise home with me."

"Any news about Richard Stirling?"

"The station was very helpful. They scanned and sent the evidence list and arrest report. Haven't had time to look at it yet."

"Okay. I'll be home tonight if you want to stop over."

Audrey smiled widely when Susan told her Lynette had made a start on the case. They savored their treats while people-watching out the window. Many of the Mom and Pop shops in this area closed at five. Susan watched the jewelry store owner across the street, and the proprietor of the rare book store down the block lock their front doors. They could probably leave the stores unlocked and find nothing missing in the morning. Westbrook was a safe place to live. Except for the occasional murder.

Chapter 10

"Mike, I'm making scrambled eggs for breakfast. And I can throw some turkey bacon in the microwave. Want some?"

"No, thanks. I'll just have coffee. I'm not hungry." He rubbed his stomach.

Susan's phone vibrated on the counter while she cooked. It was Vanessa, the preschool director.

"How's Katie? Did she wake up yet?" asked Susan.

"No. She's still in critical condition. They have her on a ventilator. But I do have some news. The doctor thinks she was poisoned."

"Poisoned? Really? But it happened at school. It was just us chickens there yesterday morning, and certainly none of us would have poisoned Katie."

"They're still trying to figure it out. The doctor said it could have happened earlier, maybe when she was still at home. Could even have been an unintentional drug overdose. He says some drugs and poisons take hours to work."

"They should look into that boyfriend of hers."

"No one knows his name. Not even her parents. No one knows anything about him except that he and Katie were constantly fighting."

"He was always just *that jerk* or *that son of a bee*."

"Lynette and her partner—Jackson I think she called him—are at the school now," said Vanessa. "We closed for the day since the police are treating it as a crime scene. I'm at the hospital now, but I'll stop there on my way home."

Susan's phone beeped. "Oops, Vanessa, I have another call. It's Lynette. I'll bet she needs me to babysit since the school is closed."

"Okay, Susan, take your call," said the director. "I'll touch base with you later."

Susan gave Mike the abbreviated version of her conversation with the director.

"If she was poisoned, what was it?" said Mike. "Knowing what poisoned her may lead them to the guilty party. You know...if she was poisoned by a farm pesticide, look at who had access to a farm and also knew Katie."

"Good point. You're thinking like a sleuth, Mike!" She kissed her husband goodbye and locked the door behind him.

Within the hour, Lynette came by with Annalise. Susan planned on taking her granddaughter and Audrey out to the mall on the other side of the river. *Shopping is the best form of bonding. Besides, I need the distraction.*

"Thanks, Mom," said Lynette. "I'll pick her up after work. Where's Audrey?"

"Still asleep."

"Before I go, can you tell me what you saw yesterday morning? You're good with details." She pulled a notebook out of her purse. Lynette's compliment made Susan sit up a little taller.

"I came in to school and one of the parents, Trevor's mom, was working on a bulletin board. Parent drop-off had finished, and Vanessa, the director, came inside. Shelley came in then with two cups of that coffee that's more like a milkshake. Mocha latte, Frappuccino—something like that. One was for Katie. Katie and Shelley had an ongoing battle over making coffee at home versus standing in line for it. We always tease Shelley about how if she gave up her daily coffee stop, she would save enough money for a vacation in Bora Bora."

Lynette interrupted, "Was any other food or drink brought in while you were there?"

"Just what the teachers carried in their lunch boxes."

"Did anyone at all pass through the school? A delivery man? The UPS guy?"

"No, not at that hour. There were two other parent volunteers besides Marin there. They were in the classrooms, watching the kids during all the commotion."

"Was Katie at odds with anyone? A parent, another teacher?"

"Yes! I almost forgot. A parent came in a few days ago, ranting about Katie stealing his son's identity to get a credit card."

"That's interesting. Anyone else?"

"She was always fighting with her boyfriend. I don't know his name. He never came by school."

"You did good, Mom. At least we have a starting point. Jackson and I are heading down to the school. Wish I'd have suspected foul play earlier. The crime scene—if it is one—has already been compromised. I'll see you later."

Susan sat on the sofa and tried to remember any details she could about Katie's boyfriend. She clenched her fists in frustration after coming up blank.

Audrey was awake. "Good morning. I slept later than I ever do." She bent down to Annalise's eye level. "Hi, precious. How pretty you look in that pink sun dress. Do we get to spend the day with you?" Annalise pulled the belt on Audrey's bathrobe.

"Lynette dropped her off. The school is closed today. Katie's doctor thinks she may have been poisoned. The police are investigating."

"Poisoned? On *Dateline* they always go to the spouse first. Was she married?"

She watches Dateline just like I do, thought Susan. "No, but she had a boyfriend she was constantly fighting with. I told Lynette to start with him."

"So what will we do today?"

"I thought a mall trip would be fun. Afterwards, we can take Annalise to feed the ducks. She loves ducks. We can go to the pond over at…." Susan stopped mid-sentence.

"What's wrong?"

"I just remembered something. The duck pond is on the campus of Westbrook Community College. Katie's boyfriend was a student there! She once said he was studying Finance."

"Do the police have his name?"

"No, I don't think Katie ever called him by name. Wasn't much of a boyfriend. She never got surprise florist deliveries or spontaneous lunchtime visits. She didn't even keep a picture of him on her desk. I wish we at least knew what he looked like."

"The police will find him. I'm going to grab breakfast."

"There's coffee made, and eggs on the counter. When you're ready, we'll head to the mall. It's about a 30-minute drive."

Audrey sat with her iPad while she ate. "Keeping up with Facebook is a job in itself. All those grandbaby pictures and happy cruise pictures. I'm going to be sure to post some of my daughter and her family."

Post some…vacation…Facebook. "Audrey! You just gave me an idea."

"What?"

"Katie went on vacation with her boyfriend around Christmas time. I'm sure I remember seeing pictures she posted. I'll bet her boyfriend is in one of them. Let me get my laptop."

Susan scrolled back through hundreds of posts. She rubbed her temples.

"Even if you find a picture, how will you know it's her boyfriend and not the scuba instructor?"

Susan grunted and kept scrolling back. Then she looked up from the screen. "Aha! Got it. And if this is her scuba instructor, her boyfriend should have been very jealous. Look!" Susan showed Audrey a picture of Katie kissing a tanned blond guy with six pack abs in a bathing suit.

"That must be him. Call Lynette."

"She's busy at the crime scene. She won't answer now. Nothing to do but wait until later." Susan sighed. "Meanwhile, I'm going to grab a snack and juice box to throw in the diaper bag. Then, let's shop till we drop!"

Macy's was Susan's favorite store, so they started there. Turned out it was Audrey's favorite too. *Coincidence?* Audrey bought two bags full of baby clothes from the clearance rack.

"I'm sure Lynette can use these. I haven't bought baby clothes in decades and forgot how much fun it is. Especially little girl clothes I never got to buy those." Susan got that *punched in the stomach* feeling. If Audrey had kept her, she would have had the chance to buy lots of little girl clothes. Audrey quickly looked away after she said it. *Does she know what I'm thinking?*

Lunch at the food court meant a smorgasbord of choices. The aroma of fresh pizza, French fries, and chocolate chip cookies gave Susan an adrenaline rush. The samples of orange chicken presented on toothpicks convinced Susan to go with Chinese. She bought Annalise chicken nuggets and fries from Burger King.

Audrey opted for a salad, however, she was all in when Susan suggested Mrs. Field's cookies for dessert.

Annalise fell asleep in the car on the way back. Lynette called while Susan was driving.

"Mom, did you say Katie and Shelley each had a latte? Are you sure?"

"Some kind of fancy coffee drink. Yes, we joked about it; remember I told you?"

"We retrieved the trash from yesterday, and there was only one coffee cup. We sent it to the lab."

"Was there one in the teacher's lounge?"

"Nope. Checked everywhere. No coffee cup. No bottle of antifreeze hidden in the supply closet. I was thinking the coffee may have been tampered with, but we only found one to test."

"I'll bet the killer took it with him. What about Katie's boyfriend? I remembered that he's a Finance major over at Westbrook Community College."

"The director had no idea who he was. We interviewed the other teachers and found what you said. They fought a lot, but no one knew his name."

"I have a picture from Facebook. I'm sure it's him. Maybe you can…"

"Use that facial recognition software that our little police department doesn't own? It's going to be like looking for a needle in a haystack."

"How about if I hang out at the campus tomorrow and see if I can find him? As far as campuses go, it's very small."

"Whatever floats your boat, but if you see him, let me know. Don't approach him."

"I won't." This time, Susan was determined to play by Lynette's rules. Before she hung up, she asked Lynette if they knew whether or not Katie was pregnant.

"I interviewed her doctor. He would have mentioned it if she was. A baby would have meant there were two victims. Did she say she was pregnant?"

"No, I found an ultrasound photo and jumped to conclusions. Never mind."

Chapter 11

When Susan arrived at school the next morning, Shelley and Eddie, the custodian, were shouting at each other in the parking lot. They stopped as soon as they saw her, but not before Susan heard something interesting. Eddie said, "I want my share." *His share of what?* Her mind ran through possibilities. *Money, drugs, vegetables from the farmer's market? It could be anything.*

Susan's imagination was already stoked by the time she went inside the school, but seeing the director's door shut sent it into overdrive. The door was never closed, and inside, she saw a man dressed in a business suit. He looked too old to be a parent. Neither he nor the director were smiling. The man was jotting down notes on a legal pad. *What is he writing? Is he a lawyer?*

She didn't notice Marin coming up behind her. "Good morning, Susan."

Susan jumped. Then she caught her breath. "Hi Marin. You look pretty today. No jeans?" said Susan.

"Not today. By next week, probably I'll be back in my Levi's. You're looking at Katie's temporary replacement. Good thing I kept my teaching degree current. Now that my sorry excuse for a husband left me, I'm glad I did."

"I'm sure the director is relieved to have you on board. Have you taught before?"

"I taught zoology at a private school for a year. I'm glad I can help. Vanessa's under enough stress, and the kids here know me."

"Who's that man in her office?"

"Not sure. I heard him say something about a bank before they went inside the office," replied Marin.

"Any news about Katie?"

"Vanessa said nothing's changed. She's still critical."

Susan took another peek into the director's office. "Good luck with the class," she offered to Marin. "I'm sure you'll have fun. Let me know if you need anything."

The morning whizzed by. Determined to find Katie's mystery boyfriend, Susan stopped at Westbrook Community College on her way home. She knew it was a longshot, but just maybe she'd get lucky. She sat at an umbrella table outside the student union building. It was still lunch time so traffic was heavy passing through the courtyard. She pretended to read on her phone, when in actuality, she'd taken a picture of Katie's boyfriend from the Facebook page and was using it to compare to the passersby. She clipped her sun shades over her bifocals, further slipping into the role of private investigator. Lynette was right about her having an eye for details. She studied each face passing in front of her. *If he was here, she'd find him,* she mused. Twice she thought she'd spotted him, but on closer inspection she was wrong.

After an hour, the traffic had lightened significantly. She bought a cup of coffee, and strolled around the campus. Beads of sweat on her brow soon cajoled her into heading back to the parking lot. She began walking in that direction when she saw him! She froze in her footsteps. A young man coming from the parking lot.

His hair was longer, but she was sure it was him. She was about to initiate a conversation, when she remembered. *Don't confront him, Susan. You promised.*

She sealed her lips together, but did a 180, following him as he turned back toward the campus. He entered the math building. For a moment, she debated whether or not to follow him inside, but then realized he wouldn't know her from Adam. She nearly lost him when the bell rang and a hoard of students poured into the hallway. *Is this what they mean by swimming upstream?* She regained her stride, and Bingo! Her quarry entered a classroom. She jotted down the time and room number. This boy apparently had a class at 3:00. From here, Lynette would be able to find him.

As soon as she got into her car, Susan called Lynette. "I have some good news for you. I'm leaving Westbrook Community College now. I spent the afternoon there and guess what?"

"Don't tell me you actually found him?"

"I did. I followed him into the math building and wrote down the room number. If you show the photo to his professor you'll get a name."

"I can't believe you found him so quickly. You didn't talk to him, did you?"

"No, I told you I wouldn't. You underestimate me, Lynette. How's the rest of the investigation going?"

"We spoke to the parent who accused Katie of stealing his son's social security number. He's been out of town on business the past few days. His alibi checks out. He said something interesting though. He was talking to one of the other parents about what had happened and they also had an issue. Apparently their three-year-old filed his own income taxes! Got a nice refund, too."

"Do you think both incidents are related?"

"Don't know yet, but for a small school it's quite a coincidence. We're working on it."

When Susan got home, she changed into a pair of comfy shorts and her *World's Best Grandma* t-shirt. Audrey was reading out on the patio.

"Doing okay? I feel bad leaving you alone here."

"Nonsense. I'm a big girl. Any news about that teacher?"

"Nothing has changed, but we identified her boyfriend."

"We?"

"It's complicated. Anyhow, Lynette's going to interview him tomorrow. Meanwhile, how about a game of Scrabble? When Mike gets home we can go out to dinner."

"Better watch it. I'm a fiend with word games."

Chapter 12

"Come on, Jackson. Let's check out this boyfriend," said Lynette. It was early and they were hoping to catch the professor in room 921 before his classes started.

"You have the picture?"

"Yep. Thanks to my Mom. I have to say, she's making progress. I'm surprised she didn't go right up to him and ask him his name."

"Good old Miss Marple. I don't know why she hasn't found a more traditional hobby. When I retire, I'm going to spend my days fishing and watching Netflix."

"It makes her feel useful. Knitting and scrapbooking just weren't cutting it."

They parked the cruiser and headed toward the math building.

"How's Theresa feeling?"

"Good. Less morning sickness than at first. We got to see the heartbeat. I couldn't believe that was our baby in there."

"You're gonna love it. Stock up on sleep, though. The room should be right down this hall. He has an 8:00 class, so he'll probably be there."

A young professor with a ponytail and beard was busy putting formulas up on the dry erase board.

"Excuse me, Dr. Lindon. Detective Lynette Green." She shook his hand.

"And I'm Detective Jackson Simpson. Westbrook PD."

He put down the marker and shook their hands. "What can I do for you?"

"We're looking for this man." She held out the picture. "He's in your 3:00 class."

"Looks familiar. Let me get out my roster." He spent a few minutes going through the lists, then pointed to the paper. "Here. Jonathan Hildebrant. Sits right in the front row."

"Can we get his address and contact information?" Lynette gave Jackson a discreet smile, while the professor looked up the information.

"Here you go. Hope this is helpful."

"Absolutely. Thank you for your time," said Lynette.

They cut through the quad, got back into the cruiser, and headed to Jonathan Hildebrant's apartment. "It's that building on the right," said Lynette. The three-story brick building wasn't a Trump penthouse, but it wasn't too shabby for a guy in his twenties, still in school. They took the stairs to the second floor and knocked on Jonathan's apartment door.

"Mr. Hildebrant. Westbrook PD. We need to talk to you," said Jackson using his deep, professional tone.

"Just a minute." The door opened and a handsome young man with messy blond hair, still in his pajamas, let them in. "Police? What do you need?"

Jackson began, "We understand you were dating a young lady named Katie Mitchell."

"We're on again off again. Right now it's off again." Neither Jackson nor Lynette smiled at his levity. "Miss Mitchell is in the hospital. She collapsed at her job and is still unconscious."

"What? Katie? Is she okay?"

"She's still critical."

"Oh, man. How can I help you?"

"Where were you Tuesday morning?" asked Lynette.

"Right here. Asleep. I go to class by day and work nights. I'm seldom up before noon."

"Can anyone vouch for you? Did you receive a phone call or talk to one of your neighbors perhaps?"

"No. I was asleep in my bed. Are you accusing me of hurting Katie?"

Lynette said, "We're just checking out all the people who had contact with her. Witnesses reported hearing the two of you arguing on more than one occasion."

"Yeah. Katie was a passionate girl. Don't all couples argue? Doesn't mean I'd kill her."

"Can you think of anyone who would?"

"Want her dead? No. Everyone liked her. What happened to her?"

"She was poisoned," said Jackson. "Think hard about Tuesday morning. Try to remember something that places you here at the time of the attack. The poison hasn't yet been identified. It's possible it was given to her earlier. Where were you Monday night?"

"I was at work at the Jiffy Mart near the campus. I worked till midnight. Check my time card."

"We will. If you think of anything call us." Jackson handed him a card and he and Lynette got back into the cruiser.

"What do you think?" said Lynette.

"I don't think he did it, but it's based on intuition, not fact. Wish he had an alibi. Young guy like that. If he wanted to kill her, he had access. I think he'd have chosen something less complicated than poison. What are you searching for?"

Lynette read off the computer screen. "He doesn't have any criminal record. Not even a traffic ticket. Oh, and I found this. A gun permit. It would have been easier to shoot her if he wanted her out of the picture."

"Now we're speculating."

"What about that parent who accused Katie of stealing the social security number?" said Jackson.

"Had an alibi, remember? A dozen people put him at that conference in D.C."

"I have an idea. Let's pull up Katie's financial records and see if anything looks out of place."

"And don't forget we still don't know where that money in the teachers' lounge came from. Katie found it. Maybe she knows more than she let on."

Chapter 13

Susan loved Sunday morning. On the weekends, Mike didn't work and they always enjoyed a leisurely breakfast together. The Sunday paper was spread out on the kitchen table.

"Do you have the puzzle section?" asked Mike.

Susan handed it to him. "Here you go."

Both she and Mike were on their second cup of coffee.

"Is Lynette coming by this morning?" asked Mike.

"Yes. She has a list of evidence from the Richard Stirling case and some photos she got from the police station where he was arrested. Want to help us?"

"Tell you what. I'll help you by taking Annalise for a walk so you can spread out all over the coffee table without her grabbing the papers." When Audrey walked in, he said, "Good morning. Heard you and the clue crew are raring to go."

"I'm hoping between the three of us, we'll notice something that was overlooked. All these years, I had no access to the evidence. Lynette got it within a day. The advantages of having a granddaughter who's a detective. Who knew?"

"Sounds like Lynette's here. I'll grab Annalise and you all can get to work."

Lynette spread the photos out on the coffee table. "These photos are what's in the evidence box. They've been sitting in the basement of the police station all these years. I'll read from the list. You and Audrey check and see if you find the item in a photo. Ready?"

"More than ready," said Audrey.

Lynette began. "Autopsy report, photo of the body at crime scene, fingerprints..."

"I see all of those," said Audrey.

"Police report, lab results from blood found at the scene..."

"Check," said Susan.

"Richard Stirling's clothing from the night of the murder, leather glove..."

"Wait!" said Susan. "I don't see a leather glove here, do you, Audrey?" Audrey shuffled through the photos. "No. No glove."

"No glove? Are you sure?"

"Positive," said Audrey.

"That's a red flag. It's missing evidence. I'll call over there tomorrow and double check. Maybe the officer forgot to photograph it. Let's keep going. Eyewitness report."

"Got it," said Susan.

"Wait a minute!" said Audrey. "There weren't any eyewitnesses."

"Let me see what you have, Mom." She read through it. "It's an eyewitness report alright. Someone reported seeing a green van pull into the Stirling's driveway right around the time of the murder. It's all here."

"Then why didn't I hear about it during the trial?" said Audrey.

Lynette re-examined the report. "Because the witness was a nine year old boy—their neighbor. The prosecution must have gotten the judge to exclude it as evidence. Kids aren't considered reliable witnesses."

"But he saw a green van. Shouldn't someone have followed up on it?" said Audrey.

"Maybe they did. Here's the name of the defense attorney. I'll try to get in touch with him, but even if he's still around, he probably won't remember details from 30 years ago."

"Thank you, Lynette." Audrey gave her a hug.

"No promises, but if there's missing evidence…"

"And if we find that little boy," said Susan. "Maybe he remembers something."

Lynette's phone buzzed. "It's Katie's doctor." She held the phone to her ear.

"Yes," said Lynette. "Are you sure? And she will recover? Thank you so much. We'll get right on this." Susan and Audrey hung on her every word.

Lynette said, "Katie's doctor said they finally identified the poison. It was nicotine."

"Like in cigarettes? What does that mean?" said Audrey.

"It means we're looking at attempted murder."

Chapter 14

The mood at the preschool the next morning was like a rainbow after a storm. Everyone was relieved to hear Katie was going to be okay.

"She's going to be okay, but someone tried to intentionally kill her," said Rachel. "I don't think we should be dancing around until we know who that is. No doubt her boyfriend is a suspect."

Susan picked up a milk crate full of hand puppets. "He's on the short list."

Shelley picked up a crying toddler. "What about the parent who came here thinking Katie stole his son's identity?"

"According to my daughter," said Susan, "he has a solid alibi."

"So it has to be the boyfriend," said Shelley.

"The police have to have some sort of evidence before they can arrest him," said Susan. "They need an eyewitness, or they have to find a stash of nicotine in his apartment. Something along those lines." She set the crate down on the rice table.

"Someone managed to sneak in and stash money in the teacher's lounge," said Shelley. "How did whoever did that get into the school without anyone seeing him?"

Rachel piped in. "No one here knows what he looks like. He could have pretended to be a workman or delivery guy. Or maybe the coffee was poisoned back at Starbucks. A random act by a psycho barista.

Remember back when someone was randomly tampering with bottles of Tylenol?"

Shelley's eyes brightened. "You're right. There was that guy who came to look at the leaky sink. Remember?"

"But, Shelley, that wasn't the same day as the poisoning," said Rachel.

"The psycho barista is a bit far-fetched," said Susan.

Marin walked in on the conversation. "What's this about a psycho barista?" She let go of Trevor's hand and he immediately ran to the slide. "Do we know yet what happened? Is Katie going to be okay?"

"We're trying to figure out who tried to kill her," said Shelley. "Katie will be fine. The police found the missing cup. It was nicotine in her coffee that did it. The sweetness of the latte must have masked the taste." She slapped her hand against the side of her head. "My God! I just remembered. I'm the one who brought her the coffee. She never stopped for it herself. It's all my fault."

"It's certainly not your fault," said Susan.

"Hmm—nicotine. Interesting," said Marin. "Look at the time girls. We'd better start class." Marin was new to subbing and didn't realize how relaxed the teachers were about starting promptly. Especially if the kids were happily engaged....or the teachers had a conversation to finish.

Susan sat in her rocker with a lamb hand puppet. She sang "Mary had a Little Lamb," pretending the lamb was doing the singing. She was no Shari Lewis, but luckily her audience wasn't picky. Afterwards, she read the rhyme from the book she'd borrowed from Shelley. The page was dog-eared. *Must be one of Shelley's favorites also.* As usual, she finished teaching while the others were having their lunch break.

Lamb. The zoo. Didn't Shelley buy a stuffed lamb for the classroom because Annalise liked the baby lamb? I don't want to interrupt Shelley's lunch. I'll go take a look at it. It would be cute to use tomorrow.

The classrooms were never locked, and the teachers passed in and out freely. Susan walked into Shelley's primary-colored room. The lamb was in plain sight, right on the bookshelf. Susan picked it up. *What's this?* She ran her hand along the lamb's belly and felt something hard. She turned the lamb over. *Someone's opened up this brand new stuffed lamb and resewn it. How weird is that?* She couldn't resist. She took a pair of scissors off the desk and picked at the stitching.

What she found made no sense at all. Credit cards. A handful of them, each with a different name on it. She rifled through them. *Wait a minute. I recognize that name. Sean Isenburg. He's one of our students! Maybe that angry parent was right. Someone around here is stealing identities.*

She rubbed her temple. Then she remembered the bag of shredded papers she'd caught Eddie the janitor bringing to the dumpster. Maybe it wasn't Katie, but Eddie who was stealing the social security numbers. He and Shelley were friends. He might have stuffed the cards in there. After all, the stitching was pretty amateur. *Did Shelley know about this? I can't imagine sweet Shelley being involved. No, it was probably Eddie acting alone.*

The stitching! How am I going to sew the lamb back up? She stuffed it in her tote bag and put the credit cards back inside. Nervous sweat dampened her bangs. She'd tell Lynette. *Maybe the police can set a trap and catch Eddie in the act. If they flat out accused Eddie without proof, he'd be forewarned and they'd never catch him.* She took a deep breath and headed toward the door.

"Thanks, Susan, See you in the morning," called Vanessa from her office. Susan popped her head in to say goodbye. The director laid down the pen she was using. "I'm so glad that Katie is going to be okay. Things are starting to feel normal again."

Susan noticed a brightly-colored gift bag on Vanessa's desk. "Did one of the parents drop off a present for Katie?"

"No, that's what I thought too. It has a tag that says *Shelley*. It was on my desk after I came in from parent drop off. I told Shelley about it, but she didn't want the kids getting into it so she said she'd grab it on her way out."

"Nice to know our teachers are appreciated."

During the drive home, Lynette called. Susan was about to launch into the credit card story, but didn't get the chance. Lynette had her own news to share.

"Mom, I wanted to let you know that Shelley's boyfriend is in the clear. The dodo brain forgot he'd ordered pizza that night. We confirmed his alibi. To top it off, the paper boy said he saw a car in the driveway the next morning. I was wondering if you knew any of Katie's friends. Maybe one of them has an idea."

"Can't say I do." A red sports car swerved ahead of her...on the single lane road. Good thing there was plenty of shoulder. "Lynette, I have to concentrate on the road. I'll call you from home."

Chapter 15

Susan had a dentist appointment after school, then stopped for groceries. By the time she got home, her hubby was already there.

Mike walked out to the driveway and began taking in grocery bags from the trunk. "How was your day?"

"Pretty good. Everyone at school is more relaxed knowing Katie will recover. I found something really interesting that I need to talk to Lynette about." She explained about the lamb with the credit cards stuffed inside.

"So that parent was right? Someone at the school *was* stealing information. Clever hiding place."

Susan and Mike set the bags on the kitchen counter. Ludwig smelled deli turkey and stuck his paw into one of the bags. "Where's Audrey?"

"She left a note. She took the train to Bayersville State to see Richard Stirling."

"What! Why didn't she say anything?"

"Guess she thought we'd try to talk her out of it. After all, she tells me George doesn't even want to hear this guy's name. Your own half-brother thinks he's guilty."

Susan stuck the ice cream in the freezer. She swore she wasn't going to keep sweets in the house, but she was dealing with a lot of stress these days. Besides, what kind of hostess would she be if she didn't have dessert in the house to offer Audrey? She'd get back to her diet after her mother left.

"Evan called. He's coming home this weekend for a visit. Wants to see his," she swallowed hard, "Grandma."

"Great. Let's get everyone over here Saturday night for dinner."

"Everyone—that reminds me. I told Lynette I'd call when I got home." She tried Lynette's number, but it went straight to voicemail. "Lynette isn't picking up. She seldom turns her phone off."

"Try her at work," said Mike.

Susan tried the station. An officer told her that Lynette and Jackson had gone out on an emergency call. *I hope Lynette isn't in danger. After all these years, my heart jumps into my throat whenever there's a possibility of Lynette being hurt.*

Lynette and Jackson zipped into the cruiser as soon as the emergency call came in.

"Jackson, the house is over there!" said Lynette. He pulled in front of a brick duplex. An officer was already on the scene and waiting for them. In the driveway, a woman was hanging halfway out of the driver's seat, door open, her seat-belt still fastened.

The officer said, "The woman in the other duplex noticed her hanging out of the car. As far as I can tell, she's not breathing. I didn't feel a pulse. Didn't want to move her before you came. I called the medical examiner."

Jackson and Lynette approached the body. Lynette felt for a pulse, then shook her head *no* confirming that the officer was correct. Then Lynette focused on the woman's face.

"Oh, my God! I know her. That's Annalise's teacher!" Lynette cupped her mouth with her hands.

"Are you sure?"

"Of course. I see her practically every day. I don't believe this."

"I don't see any blood or wounds," said Jackson. Lynette stared at the curly mop of brown hair hanging out of the driver side door.

"That's Shelley! How did this happen?"

Jackson bent down to Shelley's level. "No blood on the seat. There's a party bag on the passenger side." He ran over to the cruiser and got a pair of latex gloves. Carefully, he peered inside. "It's some sort of brownies or fudge. There's a tag that says, *Thanks for all you do for Scott each day.* Who's Scott?"

"He's in Annalise's class. He's one of Shelley's students."

"Do you think the food was poisoned? It already happened once over there. Maybe some psycho is targeting the school."

"It certainly isn't just a coincidence. There's some kind of connection. Let's treat this like a homicide until proven otherwise. Poor Shelley! Annalise will be heartbroken. So will everyone else at the school." Lynette dabbed at her eyes with the edge of her sleeve. "Snap some pictures, then we'll get the bag to the lab—stat!"

They circled the house looking for anything out of place, but found nothing unusual.

"It seems like this happened just as Shelley pulled into her driveway," said Jackson. "I'll get the camera." Jackson got the camera and took photos of the car and body from various angles, treating it as a crime scene. Lynette knocked on the neighbor's door and took a statement. There were few cars on the street, but those that passed, slowed down, rubbernecking. Jackson waved them on.

"Finally. Here's the medical examiner." The white van parked and Jackson ran to it.

"I got here as fast as I could," said the medical examiner.

"Can you tell what happened?" asked Jackson. "Or when?"

The medical examiner bent close to the body, felt for a pulse, and listened for breathing. "She's definitely dead," he said. "Looks like it happened within the last hour or so. No marks on the body. Could have been a heart attack or maybe an aneurysm. I'll know more after the autopsy." The EMTs removed the body and took her away in the ambulance.

Lynette examined the interior of the car once more. "There are crumbs in the driver's seat. She was probably eating during the drive home."

Jackson sniffed the bag and the seat. "I don't smell any poison, but chocolate is a great disguise. She could've been allergic to something in the brownies. Peanuts maybe?"

"According to the director, there were no allergies listed on her medical forms. Here's CSI. They can dust for prints. Maybe we'll get lucky. Young girl like this getting a heart attack? Really? My money's on poison."

"I'll notify next of kin. Why don't you call the director of the school?" said Jackson.

"Okay. I'm going to stop at my Mom's to tell her the news. She'll be very upset, like I am. We saw Shelley every day."

Chapter 16

Mike paced through the kitchen. "Is dinner ready yet? I'm hungry."

I'm glad he has an appetite. He hasn't been eating much these days. Maybe he's feeling better. "Why don't you set the table while I finish whipping these potatoes? The veal cutlets are almost done." Susan opened the oven door to check. "Did Audrey say she'd be home for dinner?"

"No, but I'll set a place anyway." Mike folded the paper napkins and tucked them next to the plates. "I think I hear her. You gave her a key, right?"

Audrey came into the kitchen. "Whatever you're cooking smells delicious," said Audrey.

"How was your visit with Richard Stirling?" said Susan.

"It's always hard going into that prison and seeing him behind bars. It's so wrong."

Mike said, "This isn't the first time you visited?"

"No, I've flown up here before to see him. Before I knew you and Susan lived in New York. Such a coincidence. Anyhow, when I told him about the eyewitness report and missing glove, his eyes shone like I've never seen them. At least not in the past 30 years."

"How long have you known this guy?" asked Mike.

"Seems like forever. He's one of my oldest friends. We grew up together."

"Audrey, I have to ask you again. Is Richard Stirling my father? He'd be about the right age."

"No, dear. I'm sorry, but I have no idea where your father is. I told you he planned on going to law school. That's the last I heard, and it was almost 60 years ago."

Susan startled when she heard a knock, followed by the sound of a key opening the front door.

"Mom, it's me." Lynette walked into the kitchen. Her shoulders drooped and her shirt was half tucked into her pants.

"What a nice surprise," said Susan. "Are you okay? You look like you've been crying."

"I have some terrible news."

"Is it Annalise? Did something happen?" Her heart pounded.

"No, calm down. Annalise is fine."

"Oh, thank God." Susan donned oven mitts and took the veal cutlets out of the oven. "What is it then? You sound so serious."

"Let's sit down," said Lynette. Susan and Mike followed her into the living room.

"It's Shelley." She looked at her dad. "Annalise's teacher."

"What about her?" said Susan

"She was discovered dead in her car, in her own driveway."

"Oh, my God." Susan felt the blood drain from her face. She rubbed her ear to make sure she was hearing right. "I just saw her a few hours ago. She was at school. What happened?"

"We're not sure yet. We found a gift bag on the seat next to her. It was full of brownies."

"I saw a gift bag on the director's desk as I was leaving. Vanessa said it was a present for Shelley."

"The card was from Scott's parents. You know Scott?"

"Of course. He was in her class. Did those brownies have anything to do with this? Was she poisoned, like Katie?"

"We won't know till we get the lab report. It could have been a heart attack or something. She wasn't necessarily murdered," said Lynette.

"But isn't it a coincidence that Katie was just poisoned?" Susan felt tension in every muscle of her body. She relaxed a bit when Audrey put her arm around her.

"No, I don't think it was a coincidence," said Lynette. "I wish it were."

"Do you think someone's targeting the teachers there?" said Mike.

"Who in their right mind would come after a bunch of preschool teachers?" asked Audrey.

"Stranger things have happened. It's possible. When we get the lab results, we'll start digging."

Susan remembered what she wanted to tell Lynette earlier. "Lynette, I have something to tell you that may be related. I found credit cards with the names of some of the students on them. They were hidden inside a stuffed lamb I was going to borrow from Shelley." She grabbed her tote bag from the hall table. "Look. I have it here."

Lynette took the lamb and pulled out the credit cards. "Why on earth...first a mysterious bundle of money, now this?"

"Remember how I told you a parent was accusing Katie of stealing her son's identity?" said Susan.

"You found those in Shelley's classroom," said Lynette.

Susan's eyes lit up. "Oh, so you're thinking it was Shelley and not Katie who stole the identities?" continued Susan.

"That's what I think," said Lynette.

"I can't imagine Shelley doing something like that. I can't imagine either one of them doing it. Can you?" asked Susan.

"Mom, in this job I see it all the time. People lie, cheat, do things you'd never imagine."

"You know," added Susan, "Eddie, the custodian, was friends with Shelley. I saw them arguing one day. I also saw him bringing a huge garbage bag out to the dumpster in the middle of the day."

"Custodians do that. So what?"

"I happened to look inside the bag." Susan braced herself for Lynette's over reaction.

"You did what?" Lynette pursed her lips.

"I was curious. Checking out a bag of garbage isn't a crime. Anyway, listen. The inside was full of shredded papers."

"So?"

"We don't even have a shredder at the school. Where did it come from?"

Mike, who'd been listening silently, joined the conversation. "It fits together, Lynette. If I was going to steal someone's information, I'd print it out, apply for the credit cards, and then destroy the evidence. Someone at that school has a shredder hidden somewhere, I bet."

Audrey said, "But why were the credit cards in the lamb and not just hidden in the culprit's house?"

Lynette answered. "If someone was guilty of stealing identities, they'd be worried that law enforcement might catch on to them. The first place the police would search would be their house."

"You never found out where that bundle of money came from, did you?" said Mike. "Maybe it's related. Someone didn't want it to be found."

"The first thing we'd do is get a warrant and search her house."

"Or *his* house," added Susan.

"Or *his*. And we'll search her classroom."

Lynette looked directly at Susan. "Seriously, Mom. Who besides you would think to open up a stuffed animal?"

Susan ignored the comment. "Are you going to investigate Eddie?"

"First things first," answered Lynette. "Let me take the lamb with me. When we get back the lab report, we'll know what direction to take."

Chapter 17

The preschool remained open in spite of Shelley's death. The director knew the families at the school depended on them for childcare and would be left in the lurch a second time if the school closed at the last minute. Instead, Shelley's class would be divided between motherly Rachel and Marin—Katie's substitute.

"I'm sick about Shelley," said Rachel. Tears streamed down her face. "I can't get over it. Dead in her own driveway? I saw her right before she left school yesterday. Now I'll never see her again." Susan handed her a Kleenex.

Marin said, "It's just horrible. So unexpected. Now Rachel, hard as it is, wipe those tears. We don't want the children to be upset. Luckily, Shelley had those two-year-olds. They won't understand this tragic piece of news."

"Aren't you being a bit cold, Marin? How would you feel if something happened to Trevor?" said Rachel. "Her poor parents; I'm sure they'll be flying in from Las Vegas sometime today."

"Vanessa asked us not to say anything to the parents here at school," said Susan. "At some point it'll be all over the news, but she wants to figure out how she's going to handle this. We don't even know how Shelley died yet. We shouldn't be jumping to the conclusion that she was murdered."

"I wasn't even thinking along those lines," said Rachel. "Murdered? Who wanted to kill her?"

Susan threw her Kleenex in the wastebasket and grabbed a fresh one. "It could very well be that Shelley had an underlying medical condition. You hear all the time about young athletes who drop dead during football practice because they had a heart condition no one knew about. Could be the same with Shelley."

"I just thought of something. Shelley's cats. They're alone in her house with no one to feed them or give them water," said Rachel.

"I'll drop by after school and take care of them. Didn't she rent from the neighbor in the other duplex?" said Susan.

"Yes. Yes, that's right," said Rachel.

"The neighbor must have a key. The least we can do is take care of Shelley's cats."

In the middle of the morning, Jackson and Lynette came to the school. They looked around Shelley's classroom and inspected the other stuffed animals.

"Well, Jackson. No more hidden credit cards here," said Lynette.

They spoke to Vanessa, the director, and the parent volunteers, but learned nothing relevant.

"That was a bust. Let's talk to Rachel. The director said her class is at music with your mom now," said Jackson to Lynette. "She's probably in the teacher's lounge." They found Rachel washing plastic dishes at the sink in the teachers' lounge. Jackson remained outside so he could continue to check for updates from the precinct.

"Rachel, did Shelley complain about any health problems? Headaches maybe?" began Lynette.

"No. And come to think of it, as long as we've worked here, she never once called in sick."

"Did Shelley ever mention a boyfriend or any other friends outside of school?" asked Lynette.

"She went out with Katie sometimes. I never heard her mention anyone else. As far as boyfriends go, she was very sympathetic when Katie complained about *her* jerk of a boyfriend. I got the impression Shelley had been through something similar. One day at lunch, she told Katie she'd sworn off dating."

"Do you know if she went anywhere regularly after school. A gym? The park? Anything like that?"

"No, I never heard her say anything. Wait. She volunteered at the battered woman's shelter sometimes. She collected cellphones and clothing for them. Of course, she couldn't say where it was."

Lynette jotted the information down in her notebook. "That's helpful. Can you think of anything else? The littlest things can turn out to be clues."

Rachel closed her eyes and drummed her fingers on her desk. After a few seconds, she opened her eyes and said, "She was friends with Eddie, the custodian. They ordered lunch together sometimes. Shared those foot-longs that the Hoagie Hut makes. They deliver if you order over ten dollars, you know."

"That's a good lead," said Lynette. "If they were friends, maybe he can give us some insights."

"Oh, and I heard them fighting right here at school a few days ago. I couldn't hear what it was about. They were acting friendly again later the same day so whatever it was couldn't have been too serious."

Jackson poked his head into the teachers' lounge and motioned for Lynette to come out. "The ME finished the autopsy. Couldn't find any natural cause for Shelley's death. He's still waiting on the tox screen."

"What about the credit cards? Did they get any prints off them?"

"Yes, I almost forgot. Shelley's prints were all over them. Just Shelley's."

"So it had to be her that deliberately hid them. There's another side to the sweet preschool teacher who loved cats and helped battered women."

"Look!" said Jackson. "The other teacher is on break now. Let's see if she knows anything."

They followed Marin into the teachers' lounge. Jackson spoke first. "Mrs. Weatherly? We'd like to ask you a few questions."

"It's no longer *Mrs.* My husband deserted me and Trevor last year. You can call me Marin. Lynette and I know each other already."

"Marin, we're trying to gather information about Shelley. Have you seen anything unusual the past few weeks?" said Lynette.

"I heard her fighting with Eddie, the custodian, all the way from my classroom."

"Could you tell what they were fighting about?"

"No, just a bunch of screaming. That Eddie is a sneaky character. You ought to look into him."

Jackson said, "Sneaky? How?"

"One day the director—Vanessa—was out of her office and I saw Eddie in there snooping around her desk and in the filing cabinets."

"Any idea what he was looking for? Cash maybe?"

"No, Vanessa wouldn't leave it unlocked if she kept money in there. Most parents pay tuition on line. I know I do."

"Thanks, Marin," said Lynette. "You've been very helpful. If you think of anything else, call me. Here's my card."

Jackson and Lynette walked toward the entrance. "Let's find out what's in those filing cabinets," said Jackson. The director was at her desk as the two officers entered her office. He posed the question.

"We keep registrations and health records in there," said Vanessa. "The teachers have their own list of emergency contacts, allergies, any other health concerns. They wouldn't need to go into the main files."

"What about the custodian? Would he have any reason to be searching through them? Maybe he needed a phone number for a repairman or plumber?"

"Eddie? No, he has all that information in his own office. I never see him in here," said the director.

"We'd like to talk to him. Is he in his office now?" said Jackson.

"No. Oddly enough, he called in sick today. Almost never does that."

"Can we get his phone number and address?" said Lynette. The director went into her computer and wrote down the information. Jackson and Lynette headed for their cruiser.

"I think it's time we pay poor sick Eddie a visit," said Jackson.

"You read my mind. Let's go."

Chapter 18

Susan left school at lunchtime, as she always did. She stopped off at Shelley's to feed the cats. As predicted, the next door neighbor/landlord had a key. Susan smelled cats the moment she opened Shelley's door. *I wonder if I should change the litter box while I'm here.*

She walked into the kitchen. *This is down right eerie.* A half-filled coffee mug sat on the kitchen table next to a loaf of bread, and a crumb-filled plate. Mail was strewn over the counter—some opened, some not. Things seemed so normal—as if the house expected Shelley's return at the end of the day.

The cats were nowhere to be found, but their food bowl *was* empty. Susan searched the cabinets and found a bag of cat food. She filled the bowl and poured fresh water into the other bowl. *Here, kitties. Are you hungry?* Out of nowhere, a large calico jumped up on the counter, then down to the floor to the food bowl, knocking over some of the mail. Susan bent down to pick it up. *Why did I quit my yoga class?* Her knees creaked as they bent.

What's this? A certified letter from a law firm? The envelope is already opened. She read the letter and her spine tingled. *Shelley was being sued for breach of contract. What? The letter states that she failed to honor the terms and was required to respond within ten days.* The lawyer represented an Allison and Clark Thibold, of Scranton, Pennsylvania. *What contract? What had Shelley been involved in?* She placed the letter back on the counter, and took a picture of it. She'd tell Lynette she'd seen it, but knew better than to remove it. Before leaving, she searched for the other cats to make sure they were okay.

Here, kitty, kitties! She peeked into the other rooms. In Shelley's bedroom, a tiger-striped cat napped on top of the paisley comforter. Susan sat gently on the edge of the bed, held out her hand for the cat to sniff, and pet his head between the ears. While petting the cat, Susan noticed a calendar on top of the night stand. *Glad to see I'm not the only one in the world who still prefers paper calendars to electronic ones.* She looked at the month-to-date. Shelley had written in a hair appointment, a notation that said, *serve dinner at shelter*, and in big letters, *IRS appointment*. The appointment was for the following week. *More information that might help the police.* She locked the house, gave the key back to the neighbor, and called Lynette from her car before heading home.

"Lynette, I dropped by Shelley's house to feed her cats and I found two interesting things." She described what she'd found.

"You just can't resist snooping, can you, Mom? At least you left everything where you found it this time."

"Was Shelley poisoned?"

"I can't go into specifics. We're working on it. I gotta go. Jackson is waiting for me at the station."

* * * * *

"Lynette, the ME called. The standard tox screen showed nothing unusual, but he sees some signs that she may have been poisoned. He's going to run more tests. One thing we know. It wasn't nicotine," said Jackson.

"Let's look at those bank records we requested." She pulled up Shelley's account on the computer. "I don't see any large deposits or withdrawals. All looks kosher to me. Direct deposit pay checks, rent check, utilities…"

"Too bad that Eddie character wasn't home. My gut tells me the two of them were involved in something. Can we get his bank records? Did you get a warrant?"

"I had to be very persuasive, but since witnesses said Eddie and Shelley were arguing close to the time of the murder, I got it."

Jackson scrolled through Eddie's account. "Look at this, Lynette. Do custodians make this kind of money? See the deposit there?"

Lynette scanned the record. "Here are two more. Also large amounts."

The police secretary stuck her head in. "There's a couple here to see you. They said you asked them to come in. Bettina and Mark Reiss."

"Scott's parents," said Lynette, turning to Jackson. "Send them in."

A handsome man in a suit, and a blonde woman dressed elegantly in a designer sun dress entered the office.

Jackson said, "Thanks for coming down."

"Hi, Bett." Lynette explained to Jackson that the Reiss's son Scott was in Annalise's preschool class.

"Mr. and Mrs. Reiss—I hate to be the one to break the news, but Scott's teacher died yesterday."

Bettina clasped her hands over her mouth. Mark Reiss stared at Jackson and said, "What did you just say?"

"Shelley Hall died in her driveway after work yesterday. On the passenger seat, we found a gift bag filled with brownies."

"What does that have to do with us?" said Bettina.

"Attached to the bag was a thank you card from your family." Jackson pulled a photo of the bag from a folder on his desk. "Recognize this?"

"I never saw it before in my life," said Bettina.

"Me neither. Can we see a close-up of the writing?" Jackson pulled out another photo and handed it to Mark Reiss. "This isn't my writing. It's not my wife's either. We had nothing to do with that gift."

"That's all we needed to know," said Lynette. "Thanks for coming in."

On the way out, Bettina asked, "How did she die— Scott's teacher? Did it have something to do with the gift?"

"We're investigating all possibilities," said Lynette. "I'd like to ask a favor. The director is working on informing the other parents. Can you keep it to yourselves until then?"

"Yes, we will. What a loss. Scott loved her. We all did."

Chapter 19

Mike's car was in the driveway when Susan got to her house. Alarm bells sounded in her head. Mike hadn't been acting like himself lately, and here he was, home in the middle of the day.

"Mike? What are you doing home? What's wrong?"

Mike was lying in the recliner. "I didn't feel good, so I came home."

"I'm worried about you. You've been sick a lot lately—and you're hardly eating. I'm going to call your doctor and get you an appointment right now." She pulled her phone out of her purse.

"No, I got this. I'll call. Aren't you back later than usual?"

"Stopped off to feed Shelley's cats. Shelley had a few secrets. I found out she was being sued, and she had an appointment scheduled with the IRS."

"IRS? She may have been flagged to get audited. Not exactly news you want to share with your co-workers. Neither is a lawsuit. I'd keep those things secret too."

"Me too." Susan tossed her phone to Mike. "Call your doctor and make that appointment. Now."

Audrey came through the door, sweat stains on her cotton shirt. "Blazing hot out there. Took a walk around the block and look at me. I'm going to take a shower, then I'll help you make dinner. Can't wait to see Evan tomorrow."

For a moment, Susan had forgotten tomorrow was Saturday. She felt like she'd spent the week in the

Twilight Zone. She noticed a new call on her phone, which turned out to be a message from the director. She wanted to let the staff know that she had personally called each parent in Shelley's class, and sent letters to all the other parents in the school regarding Shelley's death. She also said that Shelley's parents had arrived, and a memorial service was scheduled for Sunday.

After dinner, Susan took out her phone and laptop. *Time to check on the law firm that was on that letter to Shelley.* It took no time at all to find the law firm, which was based in Scranton, Pennsylvania. Susan scrolled through their site. The lawyers all had degrees from prestigious law schools—Yale, Harvard—pictures showed an elegant office suite. *Specialties—what does this law firm specialize in?* She scrolled through. *Corporate acquisitions, real estate, private adoptions.* Susan looked on her phone for the name of the lawyer who'd signed Shelley's letter. The one who'd sent the letter specialized in private adoptions.

Susan remembered the ultrasound picture she'd found in the teachers' lounge. *We know Katie wasn't pregnant. Rachel was too old to have more babies. Shelley! Maybe Shelley was pregnant and was arranging an adoption for her baby. Perhaps she'd changed her mind. Maybe she'd signed a contract and then decided to keep the baby. Allison and Clark Thibold. Were they going to adopt Shelley's baby?*

Susan googled Clark Thibold. *There are several Clark Thibolds in the Scranton area.* She investigated them one at a time. *This one is 75. Probably too old to be adopting a baby. Here's one who's married. Age 44. An orthodontist. That sounds about right. He has a website.*

She found his picture and bio. After more extensive research, she determined he had a wife named Allison. *Bingo! Did Shelley pull out of the contract, making the*

Clarks so angry they decided a lawsuit wasn't enough? People obsessed with children could act pretty crazy. She'd personally known a few. *Is this too big of a leap?* She wanted to tell Lynette, but imagined she'd say she was crazy. On the other hand, perhaps she'd found Shelley's killer.

"No one's answering, and the door's locked," said Jackson. They'd just arrived at Eddie Guttierez' house––the school's custodian.

"Poor, sick Eddie. Maybe he's at the hospital," said Lynette sarcastically.

"Doesn't answer his phone. No car in his driveway. Do you think he fled? Knew we'd be onto him?" said Jackson.

A blue mini-van pulled into the driveway next door. A woman with two young children opened the back and grabbed grocery bags. Jackson and Lynette approached her.

"Hi! I'm Detective Green, and this is my partner, Detective Simpson. Westbrook Police. Is Eddie Guttierez your neighbor?"

The woman shifted the groceries in her arms. "Let me grab that," said Jackson.

"Eddie's my neighbor. Why do you ask?"

"We need to ask him a few questions, that's all," said Jackson. "When did you see him last?"

"This morning, when I took the kids to school. He was loading suitcases into his car. Usually he's at work by the time I leave with the kids."

"Did he say where he was going?"

"He said he needed to get away for a while. Take a vacation. Asked me to bring in his mail, keep an eye on the house...didn't know when he'd be back." Jackson set the grocery bags on the front stoop.

"Thank you," said Lynette. "If you can remember anything else, like if he said anything about where he was going, please call us."

They walked back to the cruiser. Lynette said, "Should we have the airport watched? If he flees the country, who knows when we'll find him. Are we jumping the gun?"

"Just being cautious. He's wanted for questioning. If he isn't guilty, why's he running?"

"We're not sure he's running. He may be upset about his friend's death and needs to get away. He did call in to work to say he was sick. Let's see if he turns up at the memorial service on Sunday."

Chapter 20

Saturday. Finally. Susan had changed the sheets on Evan's bed and stocked the fridge and pantry with his favorite foods. She ran to the door when she heard his car pull into the driveway. Audrey was right behind her.

"Evan, I'm so happy to see you again," said Audrey, hugging him.

"Hey, Grandma! Glad I could get away for the weekend. I'm taking a small break. We finally finished writing the abstract for the doctor's research paper."

"I didn't realize medical students didn't get their summers off. Not until you all came to Florida last spring."

"We don't if we want to get into a good residency program down the road. How's George doing?"

"Doing great. Said to give his regards to everyone."

Susan hugged Evan. "Glad you're home. Lynette and Jason are coming over with the baby for dinner tonight. As a matter of fact, Lynette will be here in a little while. Remember how I told you Audrey's friend has been in jail the past 30 years? Lynette, Audrey, and I are going over the case. Audrey's sure Richard's innocent. You're welcome to join us."

"Sure, why not? I'm going to unpack first. Hey, where's Dad?"

Susan answered, "Still in bed. He hasn't been himself lately. See if you think he's acting strange—tired, not eating much. He promised to go see his doctor."

While Evan unpacked, Susan cleared the coffee table and turned on her laptop.

"I'll grab some pens and paper," said Audrey.

Lynette knocked, then let herself in. "Are you two ready to play detective with me?"

"More than ready," said Audrey.

"Lynette, before we start, can I ask you something?"

"Let me hear it first."

"Was Shelley pregnant?"

"No. Why? First Katie, now Shelley."

"Are you positive she wasn't?"

"She wasn't pregnant. It would have been in the autopsy report. Why are you asking?"

"I stopped by to feed Shelley's cats, and the mail fell on the floor. I picked it up, and saw a letter from a law firm saying Shelley was being sued for breach of contract. I looked up the firm. They're in Scranton, Pennsylvania. Anyhow, the lawyer who wrote the letter specializes in adoption cases."

"It's illegal to read other people's mail, Mom."

"It wasn't on purpose. The cat jumped on the counter and knocked it to the floor. When I picked it up, I couldn't help reading it. Anyway, I'm not hiding it from you. I'd also found an ultrasound picture in the teachers' lounge. Remember? I thought it was Katie's, but it wasn't. Now I'm thinking it was Shelley's."

"But we know it isn't. Shelley wasn't pregnant. Hey, let's concentrate on what we set out to do." Lynette spread the evidence photos out on the coffee table.

Audrey said, "Is it possible to find that little boy who saw the van?"

"He's not a little boy anymore. He's in his forties. I did a search during downtime at the station. He lives in North Jersey, maybe two hours from here."

"Then we should go see him right away," said Audrey.

"Not so fast. I haven't had any luck connecting with him yet. If and when I do, he has to be willing to talk to us. And, after all these years, he may not remember ever seeing a van," said Lynette.

Audrey pleaded. "But it's worth a try, right?"

"I'll keep trying," said Lynette. "Meanwhile, I did some other checking. I verified that Richard Stirling grew up in your hometown. His parents lived in the same house until their deaths. Mrs. Stirling died in 1993, Mr. Stirling shortly afterwards."

"How does that help us?" said Susan. "Audrey already said they grew up together."

"I was wondering if someone in his family could offer any additional information—about Richard's relationship with his wife, for example. I figured his parents were dead, but maybe a sibling?"

"And did you?" said Susan. Audrey looked down at the floor.

"A brother. He inherited the house and is still listed as the owner. You must know him, Audrey."

"Well, umm, let me think." She wrung her hands together. "I kind of remember a younger brother. They didn't get along back then. I doubt he knows anything about Richard's relationship with his wife. In fact, I'm sure he doesn't. They weren't close."

"We're grasping at all the straws we can gather," said Lynette. "I may need to go on over to the police station that sent the evidence photos. It bothers me that the glove is missing."

Evan walked in and gave Lynette a hug. "How's the investigation going?"

"We're making some progress." Lynette's phone rang. "I'll have to get this. Be right back." She walked to the kitchen.

Audrey said, "If Lynette met Richard, she'd know right away he couldn't have done this. I want both of you to meet him." Her face brightened. "Susan, I just got a great idea! Let's make a trip to the jail so you can see for yourself what Richard is like."

Susan certainly was curious, but held herself back. "Lynette won't go for that."

"Then you and I can go. It's not far by car. What do you say?"

"I don't know…"

Lynette came back in. "It was the lab. They still can't identify the poison. They've run through all the typical toxins and so far nothing."

Evan said, "There are thousands of toxins. It would help if you had a guess, then you could narrow it down. Lots of poisons come right from plants. Maybe they could test for ones that grow around here." He paused, then added, "Some legitimate drugs used to treat medical conditions can be toxic if someone doesn't need it. Insulin, for example."

"Thanks, Evan. I'll have the medical examiner give the body another once over. Could be we missed something that could point us in the right direction."

Chapter 21

Rainy weather set the tone of Shelley's memorial service. The quaint, stone church at the top of a grassy hill was the same one in which Lynette and Jason had gotten married. Shelley's parents were bringing their daughter home to bury, but planned this memorial service so her friends could say goodbye. The entire staff of the preschool was present, as were most of the parents. Tears flowed like water from a fountain.

"Thanks for coming with me, Evan," said Susan. He and Mike had come along for support. They worked their way up the front steps, past a bank of candles, and into a pew. The smell of incense irritated Susan's nose.

The minister, who'd never even met Shelley, painted a picture of a generous young lady who loved children and animals. *What an actor, pretending like he knew her when all his information came from a five minute chat with Shelley's parents.* He led the congregation in prayer. Shelley's childhood friends delivered the eulogy. Several of the parents from Shelley's class got up and shared memories of special things she'd done for their children. The service closed with Shelley's friend from the battered woman's shelter singing a mournful, organ-accompanied aria.

The congregation gathered in the church basement, where student drawings decorated the walls. Marin had asked the three-year-olds to draw pictures showing why they loved their teacher. Susan cried as she looked from one to the next.

"Look. That must be a drawing of our day at the zoo. There's Shelley holding the hand of a stick figure and bending down by what looks like a zebra, judging by the black and white stripes."

"The kids' lives were enriched because of her. You can see by the artwork how much they loved her," said Mike.

The rain was a light drizzle by the time the service ended and people gradually moved outside.

"I'm going to miss her so much," said Rachel. "She was like a daughter to me."

"We'll all miss her," said Marin. "What a tragedy. Has anyone heard if they figured out what killed her? Was it her heart?"

"They don't know yet," said Susan, "but they don't think she died of natural causes."

"Really?" said Marin. "I can't imagine anyone wanting to hurt Shelley. Do the police have any leads?"

"You'd have to ask them," said Susan. "By the way, this is my son, Evan. He's visiting for the weekend."

"Evan, the medical student?" said Marin

"Your mom talks about you all the time," said Rachel. "She's very proud of you." Susan noticed Evan's neck turning red and knew he was embarrassed.

"I considered medical school myself back when," said Marin. "I was a biology major before I realized I preferred learning about animals. That's when I switched over to zoology. Wanted to become a veterinarian, then a science teacher, but got married instead."

The director approached the group. "I want to introduce you to Shelley's parents," said Vanessa. "Mr. and Mrs. White."

"We're so sorry for your loss," said Rachel. "Shelley was well-loved around here."

"She told us she worked with a great bunch of ladies. That's how she put it. A great bunch of ladies. After all she went through, we were so glad she'd settled down and had gotten back on her feet." Mrs. White sniffled into a tissue.

"That no good ex of hers is behind bars. Got what he deserved," said Mr. White.

The wheels in Susan's head churned. *Shelley was married? What sort of trouble were her parents talking about?*

Two young women approached. Mrs. White said, "These are Shelley's oldest and dearest friends. They went to school together since kindergarten."

"Nice to meet you," said Susan and Rachel. "You gave a beautiful eulogy." Evan and Mike shook their hands.

"Sorry for your loss," said Marin. "My father died last year and it's as difficult as it was the day he died. Taken before his time, just like Shelley. Senseless." She looked at her watch. "I'm afraid I have to get home to Trevor. The sitter has to leave soon."

The director led Shelley's parents to the car.

Susan said, "Shelley never talked about an ex-husband. Was she married long?"

"Long enough," said one of the friends. "Guy was a no good con artist. That's why he's in jail, you know."

The other friend said, "He pulled Shelley into some of his crazy schemes."

"What kind of schemes?" asked Susan. Mike nudged her with his elbow, but neither Susan nor Shelley's friends seemed to notice.

"You name it he was into it. Illegal poker games, football pools, Ponzi schemes. The works."

The other friend giggled and said, "Shelley didn't exactly object. She enjoyed the extra money for sure, and she was always a bit of a daredevil."

"Shelley was cunning. Don't get me wrong, she had the biggest heart ever. Fed stray animals, read to the elderly. I shouldn't use the word cunning, it's more like she enjoyed a little risk. She was a charmer. Everyone loved her."

Lynette walked over to the group and Susan introduced her to Shelley's friends.

Lynette said, "Shelley will be missed terribly."

One of the friends said, "As hard as it is for us, I'm worried about Shelley's parents. Especially her mother. We'll make a point of looking in on them. Shelley would have wanted that."

The other added, "I wish she could have been here when my baby is born." She patted her pregnant belly.

"Did either of you ever hear Shelley mention a man named Eddie Guttierez? He was a custodian at the school and they were friends," said Lynette.

"No, I haven't heard that name before." The other girl shook her head. The director returned with Shelley's parents, who offered the girls a ride back to the hotel in their rental car. After they left, Susan asked Lynette about Eddie.

"Haven't found him yet. We checked with his parents. They haven't heard from him. He hasn't bought a plane ticket, so unless he drove across the Canadian border, he's still in the country."

Mike said, "What's he done? He called in sick for work; it's not like he just didn't show up."

"We just want to question him about the credit cards. That's all," said Lynette. "He and Shelley were friends. Why would he choose the weekend of her memorial service to leave town? Wouldn't you expect he'd want to be here?"

"You're the detective," said Mike. "What do you say we stop for lunch on the way home?"

Susan was happy to hear Mike was thinking about food. "I'm in," said Susan.

"And you know I won't turn down a free meal," said Evan. "Let's go."

Chapter 22

The next morning, Jackson and Lynette stood outside the entrance of the school, and questioned the entering parents. They hoped to uncover any odd credit issues which may have recently surfaced. They encouraged everyone to check their financial records and to contact the police if they found anything out of the ordinary. The director sent home a follow-up letter to the same effect.

"The parents whose children had credit cards stuffed in the lamb are coming by the station this morning," said Jackson.

"I asked the director about Eddie. He hasn't shown up and this time he didn't call in," said Lynette.

Four credit cards had been found inside the stuffed lamb. When Jackson and Lynette arrived at the station, four sets of parents were waiting.

"My son was in Miss Shelley's class last year. Now she has Miss Katie. We checked our credit report and saw an account was opened in our son's name. And it's already maxed out!" said the first father they questioned.

"When was it opened?" asked Lynette.

"In January. Just after the holidays. Did his teacher do this to us?"

"No, we believe she was totally unaware of the situation. We think someone stole the information either from her files, or from the front office. Could have even happened last year, when he was in Miss Shelley's class," said Lynette.

The other parents told similar stories. One couple knew something was wrong when they were denied a car loan, and had already filed a report.

When they'd finished questioning the parents, Lynette suggested contacting the IRS.

"I know it could be nothing," said Lynette, "but my mom saw an appointment with the IRS listed on Shelley's calendar. Don't ask."

"Pretty vague, don't you think?" said Jackson. He tore open a bag of Cheetos.

"You should try to nix that junk food habit of yours before the baby comes," said Lynette. "While we're waiting to find Eddie, and waiting for the lab report to tell us what poison killed Shelley, we might as well check this out. You're right. It's probably nothing." She picked up the office phone. She drummed her fingers on the desk. Then she slammed the phone back down.

"Did they tell you the wait time? An hour? Two?"

"I'm not waiting on the phone. I have a friend who works for the IRS. I'll try her."

"I'll get our legal ducks in a row. They're not just going to hand over tax forms."

After lunch, they received the information they needed. Jackson scrolled through. "Looks like Shelley was being questioned on tax fraud charges. More than one refund check was deposited in her bank account. Look, all these have the same address."

"Let me see," said Lynette. She checked her computer. "That's Shelley's address. She had to be responsible for the identity thefts. She used the social security numbers of the students and filed false claims. Holy Moly."

"I wouldn't be surprised if she and Eddie were working together. I'm sure of one thing. Shelley is positively guilty. Do you think one of the parents she stole from found out and murdered her?"

"They were all angry," said Lynette.

"And don't forget about Eddie. If they were in this together, maybe she didn't give him his share, or threatened to pin it on him. Motive for murder right there."

Chapter 23

Audrey had convinced Susan to take a ride to the prison and meet Richard Stirling. Susan had second thoughts.

"Audrey, if Lynette finds out, she'll kill me," said Susan.

"She doesn't have to know. I want you to meet Richard and see for yourself he isn't a murderer."

"The most successful serial killers in history didn't seem like murderers. I heard Ted Bundy was a real charmer. I hope Richard Stirling isn't playing you for a fool. This is a bad idea. Let's go get manicures instead."

"Come on. Just meet him. I know you're going to see he's innocent. Here's your keys."

Audrey and Susan hopped into the blue Prius. They stayed on the Thruway most of the trip, then exited into a rundown, industrial town. A sign said, "Welcome to Bayersville."

"Look! There's a sign for the prison," said Audrey. It's up the mountain." Even with the new alignment, it was a bumpy ride.

"I've never been in a prison before," said Susan. "I'm kind of creeped out about going inside."

"It's a little scary the first time, but you get used to it."

"How can you be so nonchalant? What if there's a prison riot and we get locked in?"

"That only happens in the movies. Besides, we won't be there long."

Susan parked the car in the visitor's lot. The air was heavy with humidity, and the sky was gray against a backdrop of evergreens. *Depressing* wasn't a strong enough word to describe the setting.

"Here's the entrance," said Audrey. Once inside, they went through a metal detector and their purses were searched. They were led down a gray hallway, which smelled like Clorox masking the odor of a dirty litter box. Susan was surprised at how noisy it was. She heard shouting and banging along the entire route to the visitor's area.

Once inside the waiting area, Susan's throat tightened. She felt claustrophobic and wished she hadn't let Audrey talk her into coming. A chill ran through her when they were led into the visitation room. *There he is, in the flesh.* Richard Stirling, gray haired, with an unkempt beard, stared at them from the other side of the glass. Audrey picked up the phone.

Audrey's eyes lit up like a Christmas tree as soon as she saw Richard. "Richard, this is my daughter Susan. The one I told you about. She and my granddaughter are going to get you out of here."

Susan glared at Audrey. She never promised they'd be able to clear him. With his coal black eyes and orange jumpsuit, he looked anything but innocent.

"Richard, explain to Susan in your own words what happened."

Richard repeated the story Susan had already been told. He came home, the garage door was open, and he found his wife dead in the living room.

"I was bowling with my buddies. Every one of them vouched for me. The police ignored my alibi. I loved my wife. I didn't kill her."

"Susan, tell him about the missing evidence. I want him to hear it from you."

Susan wished her mother would calm down. "My daughter is a detective. She went through the evidence inventory, which listed a glove. When she compared it to the box of evidence, it was missing."

"Missing? They said the killer had to have worn gloves since no prints were found. See. My case was handled like a true kangaroo court. I'll bet they'd find DNA on that glove."

"My daughter is going to check into it further," said Susan. "Missing evidence might help make a case for a new trial, but don't get your hopes up."

"I've been sitting in a cell for 30 years. It can't get any worse."

I can't imagine being locked in this place for 30 years. I can hardly standing being here for as long as we have.

"Richard, can I get you anything?" Audrey asked.

"Like I always say, baby, money talks around here."

"You've got it. Anything you need."

Richard grinned. *Something sinister about that smile,* thought Susan. *Has Audrey been giving him money all along?* She was ready to get out of there.

Outside the visitation room, Audrey grabbed Susan's arm. "So? What do you think? I told you he was a good man. Now do you believe me? I told you he couldn't have done it."

Something deep in her gut told Susan there was more to this. "Time will tell. It's hard to judge someone after ten minutes." *I got his number after the first five minutes, but I won't upset Audrey.*

They walked down the dank, gray hall and toward the exit. Susan had a sudden realization. "Audrey, this sounds crazy, but at Shelley's memorial service, remember how we found out she'd been married?"

"Yes, I was right next to you."

"I'm almost positive Shelley's ex-husband is here. She made a comment about being locked up like an inmate in Bayersville State when we were at the zoo. I wonder if anyone told him that Shelly died."

"It didn't sound like her family or the friends we met would have been inclined to tell him."

"Do you think…?"

"That we should pay him a visit and let him know?" said Audrey. "Do you know his name?"

Susan hesitated. "Let me think. Shelley's mom did mention it. It was a weird name…he was named after a state or a city…"

"Dakota!" said Audrey. "It was Dakota Hall. I remember because it sounded like the name of a dormitory."

"Audrey, you're one sharp lady. Let's head back to the visitation area."

Susan and Audrey confirmed that Dakota Hall was indeed an inmate, but paperwork had to be approved before arranging a future visit. Susan wondered if Lynette could speed things up, and perhaps come with her. Being in a prison gave Susan major hebee jebees.

Chapter 24

That evening, Susan settled down with her laptop, determined to find out more about Shelley's relationship with Dakota Hall. She also hoped to determine why Dakota had been convicted. *Did Shelley know her husband was involved in something illegal? Did she have any involvement in it?*

She googled Shelley White, then Shelley Hall. *Couldn't she have had a more original last name? There are tons of Shelley Whites and equally as many Shelley Halls. This is really frustrating. And time consuming.* Finally, she narrowed it down and found the information, or rather the lack of information, on Shelley.

There's nothing at all about her involvement in a swindling case, or any other cases. Nothing indicates she ever broke the law. She sat back on the sofa and shut her eyes. Then it came to her. *It's Dakota Hall I should be searching for!*

It didn't take long to pull up newspaper articles about Dakota's case. The first article she read summed it up. Dakota Hall had forced his wife to cultivate a relationship with a wealthy widower, who at the time was in his sixties. His wife, referred to as Jane Doe in the article, pretended to be single, and developed a relationship with the widower, Charles Kensington. Dakota posed as the woman's brother. *Jane* concocted a story about needing money to pay off a lien on her property. Then she talked Charles into investing in a vacation villa. She and Dakota pocketed all that money.

On top of that, Charles Kensington spent a fortune buying *Jane* jewels and taking her on expensive vacations. Eventually, the well went dry and *Jane* disappeared with Dakota.

Mike came into the living room. "Hey, watcha doing?"

"You startled me," said Susan. "Look at this article I found about Shelley and her ex-husband." She turned the screen toward Mike, then summarized what she'd just read.

"I think I remember that case. I'm surprised you don't. It was all over the news. The widower wound up hospitalized from the stress. Never got back on his feet."

Susan skimmed the rest of the page. "Yes, it says that Charles Kensington was financially ruined."

"Who is Jane Doe? Is she in prison too?"

"It has to be Shelley! And Jane Doe was never convicted. Maybe she ratted Dakota out in exchange for a deal."

"There's motive for you. In there with all those prisoners? Dakota could have made connections and gotten Shelley killed."

"Poisoning, though?" pondered Susan. "Don't hit men usually shoot their victims?"

"Not if they're hoping to make it look like an accident. Or that it's related to a recent poisoning at Shelley's workplace."

"I'll call Lynette. Even if I do have to confess to going to the prison with Audrey. Thanks, Mike. You may be on to something." She gave him an appreciative kiss, then called Lynette and told her what she'd found out. She braced herself for Lynette's reaction to her going to the prison with Audrey as she tapped in her number.

"Why did you let Audrey talk you into going there, Mom?" asked Lynette after Susan explained the situation. "You've never been to a prison before. Creepy, right? If you wanted to go so badly, I would have come with you."

Sometimes Lynette's voice reminded Susan of Charlie Brown's teacher in the *Peanuts* comic strip. *Wa wa wa wa wa...*

"I'm glad you said that. I found out Shelley's ex-husband is in there. I'd like to let him know that Shelley is dead—as a courtesy. Also, I think Shelley and Dakota—her ex—may have been working together in a swindling case. Look, I'll show you." Susan opened her lap top to the article about Charles Kensington. "Dakota's in prison, but Shelley wasn't convicted. Doesn't that seem strange? She was the one actually involved with Charles. Even Dad thinks it's fishy." Mike made a face at her. "Probably Shelley cut a deal with the prosecutor and Dakota wanted revenge. I think it's the key to finding her killer."

"Okay, Mom. I'll look into it, but it's kind of a leap. There's no proof a deal was made—at least not yet."

"And you'll come with me to the prison?"

"I'm not crazy about that idea, but I suppose you'll find a way to go with or without me."

Susan whined. "Please come with me. I'd feel so much better if we went together. Besides, I know how great your instincts are. If Dakota hired someone to kill Shelley, I'm sure you'll pick up on it."

"Shelley had another whole side to her," mused Lynette. "I can see how she could have been working with her husband on a swindling scam. I contacted the IRS. Shelley was flagged for filing false tax returns."

"Did one of those parents come after her?"

"We're working on checking out all the parents involved. See you tomorrow, Mom. Sweet dreams.

You'd better make some warm milk before bed. I can guarantee that prison visit will cause you nightmares."

After Lynette hung up, Mike said, "So now you know that Shelley conned an old man out of money, and put all the blame on her ex-husband. Her ex is in jail, but could have contacts out here that he could have asked to kill Shelley as revenge."

"And Shelley was involved in both credit card and tax fraud. She stole the identities of students at the school, understandably making those parents irate. I think she was working with the custodian, Eddie, who's missing. There's another possibility. If Eddie and Shelley worked together, and Shelley somehow screwed Eddie over, he could have killed her. Maybe the money came from those refund checks, or credit card advances. She could have hidden all or some of the money in the teachers' lounge so Eddie wouldn't find it. More than one person heard them arguing."

"Didn't you also say something about Shelley being sued?"

"Yes. The law firm specializes in private adoptions and I think a couple named Allison and Clark Thibold were the ones who got burned."

"What about Katie? She didn't hurt anybody. Why was she targeted?"

"Collateral damage. I think someone meant to poison Shelley, but Katie drank the latte instead. The killer had to have access to the school if he or she poisoned Katie before killing Shelley."

"The couple—Allison and Clark Thibold—didn't have access to the school. They don't even live in this state," said Mike. "And the ex-husband jailbird...even if he hired someone to kill Shelley, why would the killer risk going to the school?"

"I don't know," replied Susan, "but neither poison was detected on the standard tox screen. Like we said before, he may have hoped it would go down as natural causes and found some way to sneak in."

"Too much to think about. I'm tired. Want to come to bed?" Susan winked at him, grabbed his hand, and followed him up the stairs.

Chapter 25

Susan was convinced someone had cast an evil spell over Westbrook Developmental Preschool. When she arrived the next morning, Lynette and Jackson were standing outside a broken window. Glass littered the ground. It was still early and the students hadn't been dropped off yet, except for Annalise and Trevor. Tape blocked off the area.

Susan ran up to her daughter. "What on earth happened here?"

"The director called us. When she arrived this morning, she found the window smashed. There's a hammer on the other side. Whoever did this, left it behind. We're dealing with an amateur," said Lynette.

Jackson checked the parking lot. "Hey, Lynette!" he cried out. "Fresh skid marks. Someone left in a big hurry."

"Do you think it was one of the parents?" said Susan. "They all know Shelley died, but one of them could be blaming the school."

The director came running out the front door, holding a piece of paper with a paper towel. "Look what I found! This was on Shelley's desk." She handed it to Lynette. "I was careful not to ruin any fingerprints."

"We certainly appreciate that, Ms. Harrison," said Lynette. She read the note aloud. It was pieced together with letters cut from a newspaper. "Someone's been watching too many kidnapping movies—trying to prevent us from seeing his handwriting. It says: *The devastation you caused will follow you into hell.*"

"What does that mean?" said Susan. Why threaten someone who's already dead?"

The director spoke up. "I called all the parents personally to inform them of Shelley's death, but I didn't reach everyone. A few were out of town. Maybe someone returned and hadn't heard the news."

"Can you make us a list?" said Jackson.

"Of course," replied Vanessa. "I'll do it now. Can we wrap this up before the parents start dropping off their children? All I need is for them to see a police car parked outside."

Lynette said, "We're done here. Just keep the parents away from the window."

Susan said, "Vanessa, you can say a tree branch fell into the window and broke it last night. It was pretty windy, remember?" The director nodded and headed off.

Lynette shook her head, "Fine. Mom, it amazes me how easy it is for you to come up with a story. Amazes me, and worries me." She answered her phone as she headed back to the cruiser away from Susan.

After she hung up, Jackson was waiting and said, "What was that about?"

"You're not going to believe it. It was Eddie the custodian."

"He's back in town?"

"Who knows where he is. He wouldn't tell me. He's afraid we're going to arrest him," said Lynette.

"Then why did he call?"

"He wanted to tell us that he and Shelley worked together on the credit card and tax fraud, and *the other thing,* but he had nothing to do with killing her."

"What other thing? said Jackson.

"Guess it's up to us to find out," replied Lynette.

In the mean time, Susan had wandered back inside where she noticed leftover bits of glass inside the window, and volunteered to clean it up. Vanessa had tried sweeping it up, but missed some. *All the school needs now is to have one of the students or parents step on a piece of glass and get hurt,* thought Susan.

"Susan, we have a high power vacuum down in the basement. Eddie's not here, or I'd have him get it," Vanessa suggested.

"Say no more! I'll be right back." She descended to wooden steps, smelling the dampness as she went down. She looked around in the dim light, and didn't immediately see the vacuum. *Maybe it's in that closet.* She turned the doorknob, frustrated at not being able to open the door. *Why is this closet locked?* She felt on top of the door frame for a key, but found none. Then she bent down to see if a key had fallen on the floor below. *Maybe they didn't mean to lock it. Perhaps the key was meant to stay in the lock, but fell.*

She pushed her bifocals into place and simultaneously squinted and brushed her hand along the dusty floor. *Crawling is for toddlers. This isn't easy.* She felt something, and picked it up to examine. *It's not a key, but it looks like something that was on a key ring.* It was a green, enameled, four-leaf clover. *I've seen that before, but where?* She stood up, clenching the charm in her hand. She rubbed her head and tried to remember. *I've got it! At the zoo. Shelley dropped it out of her pocket. I'm sure it's hers, but what was she doing down here? And where's the key to that closet?* She continued to search, finding a round plastic chip not far from where she'd found the charm. *This is a poker chip. What's it doing down here?*

Looking around the basement once more, she noticed the vacuum sitting in the corner. She pushed it over to the steps and struggled to bring it upstairs. As she opened the basement door, she heard shouting coming from Vanessa's office. Someone was in there with the director. The voice sounded familiar. It was the same voice she'd heard talking to Shelley that day! She pushed the vacuum into a corner, then crept closer to the director's door. The man was loudly questioning Vanessa about an illegal poker game. His gruff voice said, "My wife spent three years in Gambler's Anonymous staying clean and then she finds this game and loses everything all over again!"

Vanessa sincerely sounded as if she had no idea what he was talking about. "The school closes at six, sir. No one's here at night. There are certainly no illegal poker games going on, I can assure you."

"You'll be hearing from the cops. And my lawyer!" The man stormed out of the office, not even noticing Susan. The front door slammed behind him, and Susan tip-toed carefully into the director's office.

"I found the vacuum."

"The vacuum? Oh, yes. Thanks, Susan."

"What was that man yelling about?"

"He thinks the school was housing some sort of illegal poker game after hours. He's nuts! I'm going to call your daughter. He's probably the one responsible for breaking the window."

Susan shifted her weight and took a deep breath as inspiration struck her. "Oh, my God! He may be right!"

"What?"

Susan continued, "Remember how I told you that I saw lights on here and cars in the parking lot one night?"

"Yes. I said we'd get the cameras fixed, which I'm ashamed to say I haven't done yet, what with all the chaos lately."

"Also, Vanessa, I found *this* in the basement just now." She reached into her pocket and showed the director the poker chip."

"What was that doing down there?"

"And *here*." She pulled out the charm she'd found. "This belonged to Shelley. I found it near the poker chip."

"Are you saying you think Shelley was running an illegal poker game in the basement?"

"It's possible. Why is the door locked to that basement storage closet?"

"It's not a closet. It's a classroom. I have the key right here." She rummaged through her desk. "It *was* here. I can't find it!"

"Vanessa, I'm thinking Shelley *was* guilty. And maybe Eddie was in on it too. I think the money Katie found in the kitchen may have been from one of their poker games. Shelley might have been hiding some of it from Eddie, or maybe she was interrupted and had to quickly stash it there behind the dishes and spoons."

"So Susan, you think this parent may be right about these poker games. Do you think *he* killed Shelley?"

"I don't know. He didn't come out and accuse Shelley specifically. I'm thinking it could have been Eddie."

"Eddie? A killer? And Shelley stealing identities and running illegal gambling right here at the school? Oh, my God! And I've been in the dark this whole time, putting our students and their families at risk. What kind of director am I?"

"Don't blame yourself, Vanessa. Shelley had us all fooled. Come on, let's call Lynette."

Chapter 26

When Susan got home, Audrey was making a grocery list at the kitchen table.

"Susan, I thought we could cook together tonight. I was watching a show this afternoon and they made this delicious looking Asian dish. What do you think?"

Susan looked over the list. "That sounds like fun. Let's run over to Shop Rite and get the ingredients. We'll surprise Mike."

The grocery store was quiet in the middle of a weekday afternoon. Coming in from the summer heat, the air conditioning blast they felt when stepping through the automated doors was refreshing. Susan and Audrey cruised the aisles for the necessary ingredients to make Spicy Chicken Pad Thai.

"Susan, did Lynette help arrange a visit with Dakota Hall yet?"

"We're waiting on the paperwork. Lynette agreed to go with me though."

"That's great! What about the missing glove? Any news?"

"Lynette said she was going to visit the police station where Richard was arrested and go through the evidence herself. Don't get your hopes up, Audrey."

"You saw Richard. Now that you've met him, I'm sure you believe as much as I do that he's no murderer."

"I know you care about him. Let's see what Lynette finds." Susan noticed a familiar face rounding the corner of the aisle. It was a young mother who'd been one of Susan's student years earlier.

"Mrs. Wiles! How great to run into you!"

Susan had to think a moment before remembering her name. "Brooke Nelson! It's been years. That can't be your baby in that wagon? This is my mother, Audrey Roberts."

"Nice to meet you, Mrs. Roberts. This is my son, Tommy. He's nine months old. It's been a whirlwind."

"What a cutie." Tommy smiled at Susan. Then he dropped the stuffed toy he was holding and began to cry. Susan bent down to pick it up.

"Here, Tommy. Your stuffed Humpty Dumpty is no worse for wear. Didn't even break his crown during the fall."

Brooke said, "He loves that toy. I don't know what we'd do if he lost it."

Tommy fussed and tried to squirm out of the wagon. "I'd better get him home. Take care, Mrs. Wiles. Nice meeting you, Mrs. Roberts."

Susan and Audrey finished their shopping and got home only to immediately busy themselves chopping and peeling at the kitchen table. *Humpty Dumpty sat on a wall...* Susan couldn't get the rhyme out of her head.

* * * * *

"Jackson, let's see if we got a match on the plates." Lynette and Jackson had spent the morning interviewing potential witnesses to the school vandalism. Unfortunately, the school was rather secluded, and the crime had happened before the staff had arrived for work. After knocking on doors for hours, they'd tracked down a witness who lived in a development down the street from the school. The man had run out to get gas and coffee before work. On his way back home, he'd spotted a dark, late model sedan peeling out of a dirt road and onto the highway exit near the school. Thinking it was strange to see a car speeding away from the road leading to the school so early in the morning, he'd jotted down the plate number.

"This is a great lead. I'm pulling up the data base." Lynette scrolled through the information on her computer, then pointed at the screen. "It's a rental, just like we thought. Here's the name. Clark Thibold."

"He's from Scranton. Wonder what business he had here," said Jackson. "He's an orthodontist."

"Wait a second!" Lynette flipped through a file on her desk. "This was the man who was suing Shelley. He and his wife, Allison. They'd hired an attorney specializing in adoptions. Let me get that lawyer on the phone."

"I'll check the airlines. Maybe we can catch him before he flies back home," said Jackson. Lynette was lucky enough to reach the attorney.

Jackson finished checking the airlines, then drummed his fingers on Lynette's desk as he waited for her call to the attorney to end.

"Finally," he said. "You were on the phone for thirty minutes. What did you find out?"

"I found out why Clark Thibold was suing Shelley, and why he was angry enough to track her down. Shelley had promised the couple her baby, then reneged on the deal."

"Her baby? We already know Shelley wasn't pregnant."

"But we also know she was a scam artist. Are you getting the picture?"

"Shelley pretended to be pregnant, signed a contract, received *mucho dinero* from the couple, and poof! No baby."

"That sums it up. I'll bet the ultrasound pictures she sent them came from a friend. One of her old friends at the memorial service was pregnant, come to think of it! When Shelley didn't respond to the lawyer's letter, Clark took things into his own hands."

"There's a flight leaving from Albany to Scranton at 4:00. If we hurry, we can catch him!"

Chapter 27

"What smells so good?" said Mike. He sat his lunchbox on the counter and gave Susan a kiss. "Is Audrey cooking?"

"Very funny. We're cooking *together*. You're going to love it."

Audrey set the steaming bowl of Pad Thai on the table, declaring, "Let's eat!" as she dished the food onto plates.

"So any more news about the break-in at the school?" asked Mike.

"Lynette says it looks like an amateur. I've been trying to call her, but it keeps going to voicemail. The director had an interesting visitor. A man came by insisting his wife was participating in illegal poker games right at the school."

"Any truth to that?" asked Mike. "You know it isn't illegal to organize a friendly poker game in this state."

"It is if you charge admission!" replied Susan. "We saw cars in the parking lot the night we drove Theresa home, remember? And when I went down to the basement today to fetch the vacuum to clean up the broken glass, I found a poker chip on the floor! And a locked room!"

"Did you tell Lynette?"

"I tried, but like I said, I couldn't reach her. If Shelley was involved in running illegal gambling, she may have enemies besides just the man who came to school today complaining."

Mike reached for seconds. "If he came to the school today, I'm assuming he's not the one who broke in."

"I think if it were him, he'd have had the conversation with the director before resorting to vandalism. Mike, are you okay?" interjected Susan. "You look really pale."

"Just tired. Feeling my age. After dinner I think I'll relax in the recliner."

"Go on," said Audrey. "Susan and I will clean up. If I can move, that is."

Mike turned on the TV, and by the time Susan and Audrey were done cleaning up, he was snoring away.

"Susan, I'm going for a walk," said Audrey. "Want to come?"

"No, I'm kind of tired myself. I want to try Lynette again to see if they found out who broke in at the school. Go on. The extra key's in the bowl by the door."

Susan's phone rang before she had a chance to try Lynette.

"Hi, George! Is everything okay? Audrey went out for a walk."

"Actually, it's you I wanted to talk to, Susan. Is Mom still carrying on about Richard Stirling?"

"Yes. She's hoping Lynette can get him a new trial. There were some inconsistencies with the evidence list."

"You have to get her to drop this, Susan! I've been getting her mail while she's been away. She's getting final notices and threatening letters over unpaid bills. I checked her bank records. She's negative. All kinds of overdraft fees too. This is so unlike her. She's always been meticulous with her finances."

"Oh, dear, George! And I know she slipped Richard some money when we saw him at the prison."

"She took you to see him? Are you kidding me? You have to discourage her from visiting that man! She's spent a small fortune on private investigators and legal consults. I'm really worried about her."

"I'll try, but if she doesn't listen to you, I doubt she'll listen to me. Maybe Lynette will find out a new trial is impossible and then Audrey will stop."

"I hope so. Thanks, sis. Tell Mike and the gang hello from me."

After this unnerving phone call, Susan once again she tried Lynette, but still wasn't able to reach her. *Humpty Dumpty sat on a wall.* She couldn't stop thinking about that silly nursery rhyme since seeing Brooke and her baby at the grocery store that afternoon. *Hey, Diddle Diddle, the cat and the fiddle. Mary had a little lamb. The dish ran away with the spoon. I've got it! I think I know where the key to that basement room may be. I've got to go back to the school right now!*

Chapter 28

Susan threw an afghan over Mike, who was sleeping so soundly, she decided not to wake him before going to the school. *I hope he's okay. It's not like him to sleep so much.* She searched for a pad and pen to leave a note for Audrey, but couldn't readily find either. *What the heck. I'll be back before they realize I'm gone.* She grabbed her keys and jumped into her Prius, then pushed the speed limit the entire ride to the school. The director had given her the code for the keypad to the school's main entrance on the night of the Fourth of July show, when she'd volunteered to come early and set up. She fished through her purse, and pulled out her date book. *Here it is.*

Susan ran through the deserted parking lot, tapped in the code, and was soon inside and in a classroom. She searched inside the piano bench until she found what she was looking for—Shelley's book of nursery rhymes. The page with *Hey Diddle Diddle* was turned down at the corner. *The dish ran away with the spoon. I'm guessing that means that Shelley hid the money behind the serving dish and ladle in the kitchen!* Next, she flipped to *Mary Had a Little Lamb.* The corner of that page was also turned down. *The stolen credit cards were hidden inside the stuffed lamb!* She found the next marked page. *Hickory, Dickory, Dock. The mouse ran up the clock. That's it! Shelley hid the key behind the clock!*

Susan ran to Shelley's classroom and yanked the clock off the wall. She ran her fingers across the back.

Oh, no! I was sure the key would be here. Next, she pulled the clock down off the wall in the lobby area. Her heart raced; she was sure that the key would be there. She turned it over, then pulled the face away from the back. When she heard the plastic crack, she made a mental note to stop at Walmart to pick up a replacement before school tomorrow. *How can this be? I'm sure Shelley marked that page for a reason. I'm not giving up this easily.* Susan searched the music classroom clock, checking every inch of it until she was convinced no key was hidden in or on it.

It has to be here! I'll bet it's in Shelley's classroom. I'll take another look. Maybe I should expand my vision of a clock. She ran over to the toy basket, and foraged through the puzzles and stuffed animals. Nada. Next she searched through the books on the bookshelf. *When Evan was a baby, I bought him a book about telling time.* She sighed. No luck. *Maybe kids don't even learn to tell time anymore. Everything they see is digital.* She was about to leave, when she spotted something on Shelley's desk. It wasn't exactly a clock, but maybe it was close enough. She picked up an apple-shaped timer. *Eureka!* Taped to the bottom, was a silver key.

In her haste to reach the basement, she failed to notice a faint glow from under the storage closet door in the lobby, or to hear the door creak open. She stomped down the basement steps as fast as she could.

Now I'll see once and for all if that locked classroom is a makeshift casino! She held her breath as she steadied her shaky hand to insert the silver key. It slid easily into the lock in the door handle. She heard a click, and smiled as she turned the handle to the right. The door opened and Susan drank in the dark, musty room.

A round, felt-covered table filled most of the space. Folding chairs leaned against the wall next to a metal cabinet. Susan pried open the rusty cabinet door and found shelves full of decks of cards, a shuffling machine, poker chips...all the props to support a night of gambling. *Who set up this place? I'm sure the director has no idea it's here.* Aloud, she said, "That man was right! There was illegal gambling happening after hours at the school. And I'll bet Shelley was involved." She heard a voice behind her that made her jump a foot into the air. She clutched her throat.

"Involved? She was the founder and CEO of Westbrook Developmental Gambling Hall." The door to the room slammed shut. Susan whirled around and saw Eddie Guttierez.

"Eddie! What are you doing here?"

"I could ask you the same question."

"The police think you skipped town. You're a murder suspect. If you hurry, you can get out of town before anyone sees you."

"A little late for that, don't you think?"

"No, no, I won't say anything. I promise." Her legs were shaking so much, she was afraid she'd lose her balance.

"I'm not having this whole racket pinned on me. This was Shelley's operation. I opened the school up, collected the entrance fees, and kept watch during the games. Nada mas. That's all."

Susan thought of sweet Katie, who almost died, and Shelley, gone forever. Fueled by anger surging through her body, she stood up straight and looked Eddie right in the eye. "And you killed Shelley! Was she cheating you out of your share of the winnings? Is that why you got rid of her? You knew she bought coffee every morning, and you had access to the school. Guess you never figured Katie would wind up drinking it. Nicotine. You smoke, don't you?" Even though smoking was forbidden on school grounds, Susan knew from the smell on Eddie's clothes and hair that he was a smoker.

"You're crazy! And should stay out of other people's business, Mrs. Wiles. I helped Shelley stash the money. We heard someone at the door after one of the games. I'd seen someone snooping around earlier that night. We hid the money so it'd be safe when we left that night. God forbid some robber was waiting in the parking lot."

"Then why did you kill her? If she turned you in, she'd be turning attention on herself, too."

"Turn me in? Like she did to that ex of hers? I don't think so." He pushed Susan to the floor, grabbed the silver key from the table and locked the door after himself.

"Eddie, wait! You can't leave me here all night! Come back!" She pounded on the door, then tried to yank it open. No luck. She pulled out her cellphone, then threw it on the felt table when she couldn't get service. She slammed her fists into the table.

What's the worst that can happen? Mike and Lynette will be looking for me, and in the morning, the school will be full of people. Wait! Who'd have reason to come down to the basement? She'd worked there for months before she realized it even existed. The hair on her neck stood up. *What if Eddie comes back for me with a weapon? What if he decides to finish me off?* She pounded harder on the door, screaming for help until she had no voice left.

Chapter 29

Audrey shook Mike, still fast asleep in the recliner. "Mike, wake up! Where's Susan? I came in from my walk hours ago and she isn't here. Her car is gone. I figured maybe she ran to the store but she's been gone a long time. Come on, wake up!"

Mike rubbed his eyes, and looked around the room. "What are you talking about?"

"Susan. She's gone! She didn't leave a note and she's not answering her phone. It's getting late!"

Mike got up, peeked into the kitchen, and called up the stairs for her. "I don't know. She doesn't like going out at night." He tried calling her cellphone. "She's not picking up."

"Do you think she's at Lynette's? Maybe she had to go watch the baby?"

"I'll call, but Jason is home at night, even if Lynette got called away, Annalise wouldn't need a sitter." He grabbed his phone.

"Lynette, it's Dad. Is Mom there?"

"No, why would she be? I just got home myself. Is something wrong?"

"She's not here. I took a nap, and Audrey went for a walk. It's been hours. I'm worried."

"Don't panic. She probably ran to the grocery store and saw someone she knew. You know how chatty she is."

"I hope she didn't get into an accident."

"Don't jump to the worst case scenario. I'll be right over."

Mike called the hospital and explained the situation. "Nurse, can you check and see if she's in the emergency room? Maybe she got sick or was in an accident." Audrey hung over his shoulder trying to hear the conversation.

"Is she there?"

Mike tossed the phone on the coffee table. "She's not there. I don't know if that's good news or bad. What if she's lying in a ditch somewhere?"

"It's a small town. Someone would have spotted her by now. How about a friend's house?"

"Nah. All of her friends are in bed by eight." Mike paced back and forth across the living room floor. "This is so unlike her." He tried calling Susan again.

"She's still not answering?" Audrey wrung her hands.

"Nope."

Lynette walked through the front door. "Is Mom still missing?"

"Yes. She'd never run out without telling us where she is."

"Unless," said Lynette, "She was off chasing clues! You know she's done that before and it never turns out well. What was she talking about when you saw her last?"

"Let's see," said Mike, "we were eating dinner, and she was talking about the break-in at school this morning."

Audrey added, "She said something about finding a poker chip in the basement."

"What was she doing in the school basement?" asked Lynette.

"Getting the vacuum to clean up the mess from the break-in," said Audrey.

"She must be at the school," said Mike. "Let's get over there."

* * * * *

Susan's knuckles were raw from pounding on the locked door in the school basement. She looked around for something to use to jimmy the lock. *Maybe there's silverware in the cabinet.* She foraged behind the poker chips and decks of cards but came up empty-handed. *I wonder if a credit card will open the lock.* She was glad she'd taken her purse with her. She pulled a Visa card from her wallet and slipped it between the door handle and the frame. *There it goes, it's starting to bend!* For a moment, she thought she had it, but it got stuck midway through. She pulled out the card and threw it back in her purse, not even bothering to put it back in her wallet.

Now what? She checked her purse, unzipping the inside pocket. *My nail clipper!* Hands trembling, she tried to squeeze the smallest part into the opening, but it was too big. She rummaged through her purse again, looking for another possibility. She even tried her own keys, which of course were too big. Then she noticed a high, tiny window. *I know deep down I'm grasping at straws, but I have to do something. I'll try standing on the folding chair.*

Nearly toppling over more than once, she stretched her arm up as high as possible, but couldn't quite reach it. *Ouch! I think I just pulled a muscle in my back.* Although her back throbbed, she tried pushing the table over to the wall, but it weighed a ton and was impossible to move.

"What if I never get out? Mike and Audrey are probably wondering where I am by now, but why would they think to look here? Calm down and think. She took a few deep breaths, then had a brainstorm. *My underwire bra! I'll pull out the wire and use it to pick the lock!* She reached under her t-shirt, unfastened her

bra and pulled it out. Ripping open the stitching was harder than she'd imagined, but persistence paid off. *I've almost got it. There!* She managed to squeeze the wire out of one side of the bra. She raced over to the door and stuck the wire into the lock. She twisted and turned it with the concentration of a safe cracker, until she was knocked to the ground by the door swinging open into the room.

"Mom! What are you doing?" Lynette, Mike, and Audrey stared down at her. She was still holding the underwire.

"I was, um, trying to unlock the door. I'm so glad you found me! Thank God!" said Susan. Mike helped her up and she squeezed him tight.

"Once again, put yourself smack in the middle of trouble. Weren't you working on not being impulsive?" said Lynette.

Audrey said, "Why didn't you tell us where you were going? Mike and I were beside ourselves when we couldn't find you."

Susan explained about the key hidden on the bottom of Shelley's apple timer. Then she told them about the whole incident with Eddie.

"Eddie was here?" said Lynette. "We've been searching for him and all this time he was here in town?"

"I don't know about the whole time, but he was here tonight. He admitted to helping Shelley open the school and to keeping watch during the poker games."

"Now you're looking for him and Clark Thibold," said Mike. "Two fugitives right here in Westbrook. What are the odds?"

"Clark Thibold?" said Susan. "The orthodontist who was suing Shelley?"

"Yep," replied Lynette. "A witness saw a rental car zipping onto the highway from the dirt road leading away from the school early this morning. We traced it back to Clark Thibold."

"You have his home address, right? Did you contact the Scranton police?"

"Of course, we did, Mom. He hasn't come back into town. His wife claims not to know where he is. Jackson and I have alerts at the airport, bus station, and train station. Ironically, he returned the rental car."

Audrey, who'd been quiet until now, said, "So who killed Shelley? Clark or Eddie? I'm confused."

"Eddie knew Shelley was dead. Someone left a note threatening Shelley on her desk during the break-in. Why leave the note if you knew the person was already dead?" said Lynette.

"I'm not following you here. Which one left the note?" asked Audrey.

"My money's on this Clark. He may have put it there to throw attention off him being privy to the murder. Especially since a witness got his plate number."

Audrey said, "So it was him?"

"He's an orthodontist," said Susan. "Must have some smarts to be doing that. Maybe he did kill Shelley, then came back to make it look like it wasn't him."

"That's either extremely ingenious, or really convoluted. Jackson and I will get to the bottom of it. I can promise you that. Let's get you home, Mom." She pointed to the floor. "Don't forget your bra."

Chapter 30

Two days later, Susan was back teaching. The broken glass had been replaced and word was the parents believed the story about the fallen tree branch. She saw Katie as soon as she walked into the school.

"Katie! I'm so happy to see you back!" Susan gave her a hug. "I didn't know you were coming back so soon! Are you feeling okay?"

"I'm good as new. I was sick of staring at the walls in my apartment. Besides, I missed the kids. I came back yesterday." A Mylar banner reading *Welcome Back, Miss Katie* was taped to her classroom door.

Rachel stepped into the lobby. "Isn't it great to have Katie back? I'm looking forward to the day the murderer is in jail, and we get back to the way things were. I mean, except for Shelley. I still miss her terribly."

"We all do," said Katie. Susan nodded her head in agreement. Katie changed the subject. "I heard the police have two suspects?"

"Yes," said Susan. "And the nicotine-laced coffee was meant for Shelley. No one was intentionally trying to kill you, Katie."

"I know. Lynette told me."

Marin, her head down and shuffling her feet, came out of the kitchen.

Susan said, "What's wrong?" She spotted dried tears on Marin's cheeks.

"It's my Dad. Today is the one-year anniversary of his death."

"I'm so sorry," said Susan. Katie gave Marin a hug.

"He should still be alive. What happened to him was pure evil. It destroyed him and nearly destroyed me. Drove my husband away too. He couldn't handle my reaction to it all. I was Daddy's little girl, especially after my Mom died. From the time I was ten, he raised me all by himself. He was my hero." Katie handed Marin a tissue to mop the tears which streamed down her face.

"Do you want to go home?" said Susan. "We can cancel music for today and I'll take your class."

"No, I'll be okay after I wash off my face. Being home alone won't help." She hugged her son Trevor before going into the restroom. "I wish Trevor could have known my father."

Poor Trevor won't even remember him. Susan's thoughts turned to Annalise. *If I died while she's this young, she wouldn't remember me. Mike and Lynette are right. I must be more careful for the sake of my family.*

"It's time to start the day," said Katie. She herded her kids into the classroom, squeezing Trevor's hand as she did.

Lynette and Jackson parked in front of the Westbrook Inn, where they'd established that Clark Thibold was staying.

"I say we go in after him," said Jackson.

"Give it a few more minutes."

"I haven't had a chance to talk to you this morning. I found out some key information. I talked to his lawyer earlier. Clark says that Shelley promised them her baby. Problem is, Shelley denied it."

"They must have had a contract," said Lynette.

"Nope. They didn't have an official agreement. Just a verbal deal."

"How crazy is that?" said Lynette. "Did they pay her anything?"

"Lawyer says Clark claims he sent her a truckload of cash, and the remainder was due on delivery, no pun intended."

"So even though the lawyer sent the letter to Shelley, they were basically just bluffing?"

"You got it."

"No wonder Clark came to see her in person. He must have been furious."

"Furious enough to kill," said Jackson. "Only here's the kicker. This wasn't Clark's first trip here. He bought a round trip ticket to Westbrook about a month ago. I verified it with the airline. He was on those flights."

"*Before* Shelley died?" Lynette scratched her head.

"The day before she died."

"Are you kidding me? But what about the day Katie was poisoned. Was he here then?"

"No record that he flew, but he might have driven here. He was away at a dentist conference during that time. The conference was in North Jersey. That's within a few hours' drive."

"Hey, isn't that him?" said Lynette.

"Sure is. He doesn't know we're detectives. Let's approach slowly so we don't scare him off."

Lynette and Jackson walked across the street and were soon face to face with Clark Thibold. Jackson pulled out his badge and said, "Mr. Thibold, you're just the man we were looking for. We need your help. We have to ask you a few questions."

Chapter 31

"I don't understand. What would I know that would help a couple of detectives? Do we need to go down to the station?"

"Yes, but we won't take too much of your time." They drove to the station in silence. Lynette led the way to her office, and pulled an extra chair over to her desk.

"We have a few questions about an ongoing investigation, that's all," said Jackson. "I'm sure you want to help us any way you can. It's not an interrogation. We're just having a friendly chat. Can I get you some coffee?"

"Why are you here in Westbrook, Mr. Thibold? It's a long way from Scranton," said Lynette.

"I came to meet with someone about a business deal."

"What sort of business deal?" asked Jackson.

"It's confidential." Jackson and Lynette stared at him until he began to squirm in his seat. "It's personal. My wife and I have been trying to start a family for over a decade. We hired a surrogate who lives here in Westbrook."

"Is it typical, meeting with a surrogate before the birth? My understanding is that lawyers generally handle the details, especially when the surrogate lives out of town," said Jackson.

"We had communication issues. I came to clear things up. My poor wife is a wreck worrying the surrogate is going to pull out. She hasn't returned any of our calls."

"And did you find her? The surrogate, I mean. Did you clear up the problem?"

"No. I tried her home, then I even tried her workplace. I couldn't connect with her."

Jackson leaned closer. "So you came out here again, went to her workplace, threw a hammer through the window, and left a threatening note on her desk."

"What are you, crazy? How dare you! I refuse to say another word without my lawyer present. I'm done cooperating."

"You're free to leave, Mr. Thibold. We're not holding you," said Lynette.

"But I'm sure we'll meet again," said Jackson. Mr. Thibold pushed the chair hard against the desk as he left Lynette's office.

"Well? What do you think?" said Jackson.

"I'm sure he broke the glass and left the threatening note on Shelley's desk. What I don't know is if that was all a cover up. Did he come back to Westbrook to make it look like he didn't know Shelley was dead?"

"Maybe he came to find proof that they'd made a deal with Shelley." Jackson's phone vibrated. "It's my buddy at the Scranton station. He was going to swing by and question Allison Thibold." Jackson put the phone on speaker.

"Hey, Jacky! I had a chat with Mrs. Thibold this morning. The woman's a basket case. Says her hubby is away on business. The living room was full of baby stuff. I asked if they had children and she starts bawling, going on and on about how they are supposed to be adopting a baby but she's afraid it won't happen. She starts getting wobbly, so I go and get her a glass of water from the kitchen. Right there on the counter was a bottle of Xanax."

"She believed her husband was away on business?" said Jackson.

"Seemed to. Anyhow, after I left, I did some checking. Two days ago, Allison Thibold was taken to the emergency room. Thought she was having a heart attack. Turned out it was a panic attack. It wasn't the first time."

"But she's home now."

"Yeah. They sent her home the same night."

"Thanks, pal."

"No problem. You'd do the same for me. Hey, I expect a birth announcement and a few pics when that baby comes. Still can't believe you're gonna be a dad. Better you than me."

"You're on the short list. Talk to you soon."

Lynette poured herself a cup of coffee. "It's nice to have friends. If Allison is as much of a basket case as your buddy says she is, I just had a thought…"

"You and me both. Let's find out if Allison Thibold has an alibi for the day Katie was poisoned, and the day Shelley was murdered."

Chapter 32

"Mom, it's me. Jackson and I have to go out of town unexpectedly tomorrow. Can you pick up Annalise after school and watch her till Jason gets done teaching?"

"Of course. By the way, did you ever check on visiting Dakota Hall? I know there's something more to the story about why he's there. He could shed more light on Shelley's true colors."

"Maybe I should go alone."

"No, Lynette. He'd wonder why a detective was visiting him. At least I can tell him I was a friend of Shelley's and wanted to let him know about her death."

"Whatever. I'll set something up for next week."

"Thanks, Lynette. Where are you going, anyway?"

"Scranton. We'll be home tomorrow night."

While packing up to leave for the day, Susan noticed Marin standing in the doorway. "Marin, are you feeling any better?"

"Not really. I keep thinking about my Dad. Did I hear you talking to Lynette? Is she going someplace?"

"Yes, to Scranton to follow up on a lead. A man was identified leaving the school shortly after the break in."

"Do they think he killed Shelley?"

"Let's just say he's a person of interest."

"You know, the day Shelley was killed, I saw a stranger in the director's office while she wasn't there. I'd forgotten about it. Come to think of it, didn't the director say she noticed the gift bag on her desk after she came back from lunch? I'll bet it was him. I'll bet it was the same person. I wish we had a picture of him."

"Hey, I do! There's one on his webpage." Susan searched on her phone. "Look, here he is! Clark Thibold, orthodontist."

Marin peeked over her shoulder. "That's him! That's the man I saw."

"This is great. Let me call Lynette. Wait, she's on a flight to Scranton. I'll have to catch her later. This is an important clue."

"Glad I could help." Marin glanced at her watch. "I've got to get going now too. I have a lunch meeting over at the zoo. We're planning the grand opening of the rainforest exhibit."

"Annalise and I will be there with bells on. Let me know the date."

Jackson and Lynette walked into the Scranton police station, and were directed to Jackson's buddy's office.

"Not too shabby," said Jackson. "Art work on the lobby walls? Looks more like a hotel than a station."

"It's all about ambience. Hey, Jacky boy. It's good to see you in the flesh. A little more flesh than I remember," said the detective. He pointed to Jackson's paunch.

"Yeah, well, marriage packs the pounds on you."

Lynette interjected, "Come on now, *Jacky*. Theresa's a good cook, but you had that Santa Claus belly long before you met her."

"Thanks a lot, Lynette. Partners are supposed to be on the same team. By the way, Sal, Lynette. Lynette, Sal."

"Great to meet you. We really appreciate your help. And Jackson, you have to lose that belly if you want to chase around after your kid."

"Ah, you can start your diet tomorrow. Help yourself to the coffee and croissants. Come on into my office." Jackson picked up a sugar-coated croissant. They followed Sal into a large office, with a polished wooden desk, and cushioned chairs.

"Were you able to track down toll records on Allison Thibold?" said Jackson.

"Just got them a few minutes ago. Let's see..." Sal flipped through the report. "Bingo. Allison Thibold took the toll road out of Scranton the day before your teacher friend was poisoned, *and* the day before the victim was killed. Came back the next day. We got her exiting as close as a toll road can get you going into Westbrook."

"You can't be sure it was her and not her husband though. Not if we're going just by the plates."

"We can check the gas stations and rest stops along the way. It's a long ride. She or he wouldn't have made it on a tank of gas. We should start with the Super Walmart. People tend to stock up on a few things before a long road trip."

Lynette said, "You must have your own work to take care of, Sal. Jackson and I can check it out if you lend us a car."

"You can borrow a cruiser. Do you want me to call Allison Thibold down to the station?"

"Let's see if we can gather some receipts first," said Jackson. "Maybe some security footage. The more we have on her, the more leverage we have to get her to talk."

Lynette handed Sal the letter from the lawyer. "What's the quickest way to get to this guy's office?"

"It's just a few blocks from here. I'll jot down directions."

"Thanks, Sal."

Lynette and Jackson got behind the wheel of the cruiser. Lynette checked her phone.

"It's a message from my mom," said Lynette. "She says Marin down at the preschool remembers spotting a man in the director's office right about the time we think the gift bag was left for Shelley."

"Why didn't she mention it earlier?"

"Mom says she just now remembered. Anyhow, turns out it *was* Clark Thibold. Marin identified him from the picture on his website."

"So both Allison and her hubby made suspiciously timed trips to Westbrook. We think Allison took the toll road the day before Katie drank the poison coffee. A witness places Clark Thibold in the director's office right around the time the poison brownies were left there for Shelley. Clark also took a flight *after* Shelley was killed. Which one is guilty?"

"How do we know they weren't working together? Watch out. Make a left at the light."

Chapter 33

Carlton, Russ, and Associates was housed in a three-story, brick office building set back off a main thoroughfare. White shutters and trim coupled with the large, shady maple trees at the entrance stated trustworthiness, and charm. Lynette and Jackson scanned the wall directory, then took the elevator to the third floor.

Jackson led the way. "Looks like this guy's done pretty well for himself. He's got the entire third floor to himself."

"Not too far off from our offices at the station." Both she and Jackson suppressed laughs. Lynette hit the buzzer on the glass door to the office suite. "Here goes."

Statuesque, with salt and pepper hair, John Carlton appeared to be in his late forties or early fifties. Lynette extended her hand.

"Mr. Carlton, I'm Detective Lynette Green, and this is my partner, Jackson Simpson. We're with the Westbrook, New York P. D."

"How can I help you?"

"We're working on a murder investigation. The victim, Shelley Hall, received a letter from your firm. Your clients, Allison and Clark Thibold, threatened a law suit. Does that ring a bell?"

"I can't discuss my clients. Being in law enforcement, I'm sure you understand."

"We have a warrant for the records. A young preschool teacher with ties to your clients was murdered. Another was poisoned. We'd appreciate your cooperation."

Mr. Carlton glanced at a picture on his desk. It showed him dancing with a young woman in a wedding gown, presumably his daughter. "What do you want to know?"

Jackson began. "Both the Thibolds were in Westbrook recently. Allison Thibold was in town at the time the first teacher was poisoned."

Lynette said, "And Clark Thibold was there twice. He was in town at the time of the second teacher's murder, and again after the murder. We suspect he threw a hammer through the window of Ms. Hall's workplace and left a threatening note on her desk, even though she was already dead."

"That doesn't sound at all like him. I found him to be quite level-headed. Mrs. Thibold, on the other hand. She was extremely emotional. Especially when she realized that the woman she was counting on to give them her child, had backed out of the deal."

"Didn't you prepare a contract beforehand?" said Lynette.

"No, they came to me after they were already dealing with Ms. Hall. They sought legal help only after they realized something was wrong. There *was* no contract. We couldn't even prove that Ms. Hall had promised them her baby, or in fact that she was even pregnant. The letter was a bluff. My clients tried repeatedly to contact Ms. Hall, but she refused to reply. They were infuriated."

"There wasn't any recourse?" said Jackson.

"Not without some kind of proof. Perhaps that's what the Thibolds were after when they came to Westbrook."

"Thank you for your cooperation. We'll be in contact if we have further questions." Jackson led Lynette out of the office.

"Let's follow up on the receipts. Want to start at the Super Walmart?"

"Sure," said Lynette. "With the toll records and a few receipts, we can bring the Thibolds in for questioning."

"So far, all the parents affected by Shelley's credit card and tax scams are clean. No prior arrests, and all had alibis. We've eliminated the husband who was mad about his gambling wife. He had an airtight alibi. Eddie the custodian is still missing. We haven't ruled him out, especially since he locked your mother in the basement, and admitted to working the poker scam with Shelley."

"Maybe Eddie fled simply because he was scared and didn't kill Shelley after all."

"He claimed to be in love with her, and they were making a nice little profit together. I say he and the Thibolds are at the top of our suspect list," said Jackson. He drove to the Super Walmart, where their search came up empty.

"That was a waste of time," said Lynette.

"Not a total waste," said Jackson. He tore open a bag of Cheetos. "Want some?"

"What is it with you and orange food?" said Lynette.

"I felt my blood sugar dropping. These hit the spot."

"This was dumb. Allison or Clark Thibold wouldn't have taken the time to stock up for a road trip! Let's move on to the gas stations," said Lynette.

They stopped at three different gas stations, finding no valuable clues. Lynette suggested heading back to the Scranton Police Station.

"Let's try one more," said Jackson. "Sal's working on getting receipts from the ones closer to Westbrook. They had to have filled up before getting on the toll road. No one pays premium gas prices at the rest stops given a choice of filling up in town."

"Okay, I need a bathroom break anyway."

The manager at their next stop sat behind glass at the cashier stand. "Can I help you?"

Lynette said, "Westbrook police. We need receipts and security footage to help us with a case we're working on." She handed him a note with the dates and names in question.

"Sure. Give me a minute." He assembled the records and gathered the security footage. "Come into my office."

Lynette flipped through the receipts for the days they were looking at. "Here it is! Allison Thibold used her credit card here to fill up her car the day before Katie was poisoned!"

"Did she happen to buy a bunch of cigarettes or nicotine patches?" said Jackson.

"No such luck. Just a jumbo coffee and the gas."

"Keep going. Check out the day before Shelley was murdered."

Lynette weeded her way through the stack of receipts. "Here we go! A credit card in both their names was used to fill up the day *before* Shelley died."

"But who used the card? Was it Allison or Clark making the trip the second time?"

The manager pointed to the security monitor. "You can check the tape. It might answer your question."

Jackson and Lynette glued their eyes to the fuzzy images on the screen. "There! Freeze it," said Jackson.

"Well, what do you know? It's our old friend, Clark Thibold. Wasn't the dental convention in the opposite direction?"

"Yep," said Lynette. "I think it's time Sal brings in the Thibolds for a little chat."

Chapter 34

Sal separated the Thibolds. He, Jackson, and Lynette brought Clark into the interrogation room, while Allison waited outside.

Clark Thibold looked back and forth between Lynette and Jackson. "What are you two doing here in Scranton? Are you following me?"

"We had a few more questions, that's all. Mr. Thibold, where were you the evening of July 22?" said Jackson.

"I was away at a dental convention."

"We know that's a lie," said Jackson. "We have receipts showing you took the toll road into Westbrook that day. It was the day before Shelley Hall was murdered."

"Who's Shelley Hall?"

"Don't even go there. We know you and your wife had an agreement with her. You were going to adopt her baby. When she pulled out of the deal, you and your wife were furious, and you drove out to Westbrook to kill her."

"No, that's not true! We were upset, no doubt, but I'm no murderer."

"We know you never checked in at that dental convention. And why did you enter into an agreement without a contract? Why not go through a legitimate agency? Educated man like you should have known better."

"We couldn't. My wife's medical history disqualified us. Believe me, we tried that route."

"Medical history?"

"She...she had a series of hospitalizations. For mental illness. The agencies wouldn't approve her. A surrogate was our only hope. Allison's mental breakdowns occurred first when we couldn't conceive, then later when we went through fertility treatments. Such a roller coaster ride. She did get pregnant. Twice. We lost the baby both times. Wouldn't that drive anyone to the brink of insanity?"

Jackson leaned forward. "So Shelley Hall was the straw that broke the camel's back, yet again. Must be hard, seeing your wife go through such pain. You went to Westbrook, found Shelley Hall, and murdered her for what she'd put you and your wife through. I understand. Probably woulda done the same had it been me."

"You got it wrong. This was our last hope. Allison was so excited. We even got an ultrasound picture in the mail from Shelley which is still on our refrigerator." He sighed and looked down. "Okay...I did go to Westbrook and I did find Shelley Hall, but I only talked to her. Tried to reason with her. I saw I was getting nowhere, so I turned around and went home. End of story."

"Where did you speak to her? Did anyone see you?"

"I found out she worked at a preschool. I went over there a little after six, when just about everyone was gone. We spoke in the lobby."

"So no one saw you?"

"No, no one. Wait a minute! There was a woman there with a little boy. I think she worked there. Because she came out of one of the classrooms. She saw me leave. She can verify that Shelley Hall was alive when I left."

Lynette broke into the conversation. "Ms. Hall wasn't murdered that night. Someone brought a gift bag to the main office for her the next day. It contained poisoned brownies. Don't you have access to various drugs in your practice? Drugs that, in excess, could kill someone if say, they were stirred into a batch of brownies?"

"What drugs? I put metal bands and wires in people's mouths. It's not like I'm an oral surgeon. Total fiction! I was upset, had too much to drink that night. Slept it off and went back home the next day. I'm done talking. I want a lawyer."

"Fine. Meanwhile, we'll see what your wife has to say," said Jackson. He escorted Mr. Thibold out of the station while Sal brought in Allison Thibold.

Lynette started the conversation. "Mrs. Thibold, I understand you suffered a great disappointment. You were expecting to adopt a child and the birth mother didn't follow through with the deal."

"That's right. So what? Did you bring me here to discuss my disappointment?" You came a long way for that."

"We're dealing with a murder and an attempted murder. We have proof that you were in Westbrook at the time a young preschool teacher was poisoned. She happens to work at the same school as the woman who promised you her baby."

"I've never been …"

"You can cut out the act," said Jackson. "We have receipts proving you drove to Westbrook the day before the poisoning."

Allison Thibold fumbled in her purse, taking out a pack of cigarettes.

"What a coincidence. You smoke, and the teacher was poisoned with nicotine," said Jackson.

"All right. I'll admit I was in Westbrook. I went to talk to Shelley Hall, to try to convince her I'd be a good mother. Know what she told me? She admitted she wasn't even pregnant! I was madder than I can put into words, but I didn't try to kill anyone."

"You were at the school that morning and slipped nicotine into the coffee that you expected Ms. Hall to drink."

"Morning? I spoke to her in the evening. I never went to the school in the morning and I can prove it."

"Go on," said Lynette.

"After talking to Ms. Hall, I was so upset, I had a major panic attack. I spent the night at the hospital. They didn't let me out till practically lunch time. You can check. Call the hospital."

Lynette stepped out and called Westbrook General. They confirmed that Allison Thibold was indeed there at the time of the poisoning. All eyes were on Lynette when she came back into the interrogation room. "Well, Mrs. Thibold. Looks like you have yourself an alibi. You're free to go."

Chapter 35

Jackson and Lynette landed in Westbrook shortly after sundown.

"I can't wait to get back to Annalise. Wait and see how much you miss your baby if you have to go out of town." Lynette drove to her mother's house.

"She missed you," said Susan. Annalise reached for her mother.

"She was such a good girl. We took her to Chuckie Cheese for dinner. I don't know who had a better time, Annalise or Dad."

"And the pizza wasn't bad," said Audrey. "Did you find the information you were looking for in Scranton?"

"Allison has an alibi for the time Katie was poisoned. Clark Thibold lawyered up. He's still on the short list."

"And Eddie?" said Susan. "Have you found him yet?"

"No, but we have a lead. He's on our radar too."

"We're still on for tomorrow afternoon, right? We have an appointment to visit Dakota Hall at the prison. We're still going, aren't we?" said Susan.

Lynette sighed. "Yes, against my better judgment, we're going together. If Shelley screwed her husband over as badly as it seems, he has a strong motive and the right connections to have had her killed."

"So you're thinking the killer was either Clark Thibold, Eddie, or someone hired by Shelley's ex-husband," said Audrey. "Do we know what the poison was yet?"

"They've narrowed it down to a neurotoxin, but they're still working on identifying the exact one. Mom, I'll pick you up at 1:00."

Chapter 36

After chasing Annalise around Chuckie Cheese for a couple of hours, Susan had slept like a log. The early morning phone call woke her up with a jolt. It was Lynette. Susan heard Annalise crying in the background.

"Mom, I think Annalise has an ear infection. She was up crying half the night. We're going to have to reschedule the prison visit," said Lynette.

"She sounds miserable, poor baby. Go on and get her to the doctor. Call me afterwards. Give her a kiss for me."

Susan heard the shower running. She slipped into her pink slippers and padded downstairs to start the coffee and surprise Mike with eggs and toast. Ludwig and Johann followed her into the kitchen, and waited patiently while she shook Meow Mix into their bowls. Mike, dressed for work, came into the kitchen a little while later.

"I smell coffee," said Mike. "Eggs too? You shouldn't have."

"A special treat for my hubby."

Mike took a plate of crusty scrambled eggs to the table, where he washed down each bite with a swig of orange juice. "Are you and Lynette going to the prison today?"

"No, Annalise is sick. We'll have to reschedule. Maybe I'll spend the afternoon with Audrey. I was thinking I could take her to the Joshua Tree for lunch, then we can explore the antique shops over in Redbourn."

"Sounds like a nice afternoon. Better than spending it in a prison, for sure. I gotta go. See you tonight." Mike gave her a kiss, then grabbed his lunchbox.

"You didn't finish your eggs."

Mike patted his stomach. "I had plenty. I'm stuffed."

It isn't like him to leave food on his plate. I'm starting to worry. Come here, kitties. Susan put Mike's plate on the floor, and the cats delicately nibbled up the breakfast leftovers. Susan reached down to pet Ludwig. "At least you and Johann like my cooking."

Susan thought about the change in plans. On the one hand, lunch and shopping with Audrey would be a pleasant alternative to her original plans. On the other hand, it had taken weeks for Lynette to schedule the prison visit. Her gut told her talking to Dakota Hall would shed light on the likelihood of him having hired someone to kill Shelley. Lynette had verified that Shelley had cut a deal with the authorities. By blaming the entire swindling plot on her husband, she'd avoided prison time. Dakota had to be furious. That left him, Eddie, and Clark Thibold as prime suspects in Shelley's murder. *I can do this,* thought Susan. *I can go to the prison by myself and talk to Shelley's ex. Poor Lynette has a hectic schedule as it is, and now with Annalise sick...*

After finishing her teaching for the day, she stopped at a McDonald's and grabbed lunch on her way to Bayersville State. The drive seemed shorter now that she'd already been there once. The sky turned gray and it started drizzling as Susan pulled into the visitor's parking lot. The sight of the barbed wire fence and lookout tower made her shudder.

She checked in at the front desk, and was led to the first security checkpoint by a serious-looking guard with dark, wavy hair and a beer belly.

"Ma'am, empty your pockets and place your phone and purse on the belt."

"I'm here to see a co-worker's husband. A deceased coworker's husband. Ex-husband, actually. I don't know him personally. Can't say I know any prisoners personally. The people I associate with aren't that sort..."

"Ma'am, please put your things on the conveyer." He hooked his thumbs into his belt loops.

"Yes, sir."

She was escorted through another security check before being led to the visitation area.

"Guard, what's all that banging and yelling I hear? The prisoners are in their cells, right? You wouldn't be letting them mingle with us civilians, right?"

"No, ma'am. Everything is under control."

"Are you sure? Because I don't want to come face to face with any prisoners, except the one I'm here to see, of course."

"It's under control."

Susan's nose itched. The prison smelled bleachy clean, but if you had a delicate nose like she did, the faint stench of urine and sweat broke through.

"I'll be right outside," said the guard.

The cement-walled visitor's area was sterile. Several visitors were already seated when Susan walked in. She scanned the other visitors. *I wonder who that woman came to visit. Looks like her son. I wonder what he did to get in here.* The prisoners entered through a separate door on the other side of the glass.

Susan was thankful for the glass separating her physically from the prisoners. She sat on a hard chair between two other visitors, flanked by wooden partitions—a poor attempt at providing study carrel-style privacy. The woman next to her was talking to a monster-sized man with a scraggly beard and tattoos all over his arms. *I'll bet he's in here for murder.* She shuddered. She'd been nervous when she'd met Richard Stirling, but at least Audrey had been with her. Her stomach fluttered as Dakota Hall took a seat on the other side of the glass.

Shelley's ex looked like a young Brad Pitt. *Given a decent haircut and a shave, he could be modeling underwear or hawking a designer fragrance.* Her stomach calmed down.

Dakota picked up the phone. "So who are you? When they said I had a visitor, I couldn't imagine who it'd be. No one comes to visit me—ever. You must want something. I only agreed to meet with you to break up the boredom. They said there were two of you."

"My daughter was supposed to come along but had a change of plans. Mr. Hall, you don't know me. I worked with your ex-wife. In fact, my granddaughter was in her preschool class."

"My ex? You mean Shelley, that lying whore?"

"Um, yes. She'd be the one."

Dakota covered his left ear with his hand. "I never want to hear that name again. What are you doing here? Any friend of Shelley's ain't a friend of mine. I have nothing to say to you."

Susan cleared her throat. "As a courtesy, I came to inform you that Shelly is dead. I figured you wouldn't hear it from her family. Thought you might want to know."

"Dead? What?" Dakota scratched his head.

"Shelley's neighbor discovered her dead in her car, right in her driveway, in broad daylight. She's going to be buried near her family, in Las Vegas. I met Shelley's parents at the memorial service. That's how I found out she'd been married to you. I'm sorry for your loss," said Susan.

"Sorry? Lady, you've just made my day! I'm in here because of her, you know. Frick'n con-artist, that's what she was. She drags me into her get rich quick scheme, then turns on me. Rats me out to the police. I wind up in here, and she flies away, free as a bird. Don't be sorry."

"I don't know anything about that. You must have hated her. I'll bet you'd have killed her yourself given the chance."

"I'll spare you the details. Thanks for bringing me a ray of sunshine." Dakota stood up, and a guard led him away.

Well, they were divorced...even so, his reaction wasn't what I expected. Con-artist. Her friends called her that too. Interesting girl. Susan suddenly wished Lynette had been there. Would she think Dakota was capable of hiring a hit man? She couldn't wait to get out of this dungeon and discuss it with her.

The guard with the beer belly led her back through the first security area. "Sir, let me ask you something. Don't you think even if a person is divorced, and even if his ex-wife did something terrible, he'd still show some amount of grief when he found out she was dead?"

"Don't know, ma'am. Follow me."

"Why do they have two checkpoints? Is it really necessary?"

"Prison rules, ma'am."

It was a long walk to the next check point, where she'd get her purse and phone back. It seemed even longer as the guard wasn't inclined toward small talk. As they were about to exit the first area, all of a sudden alarms blared and the metal doors on either side of the room slammed shut. The hair on Susan's neck stood up. She covered her ears to protect them from the piercing sound, realizing the gravity of the situation. She was trapped!

She grabbed the guard's arm. "Guard, what's happening? Why did they lock us in? What are the sirens for?"

The guard extricated his arm from Susan's grasp. "Calm down, ma'am. They'll search the place, break up whatever fight or escape attempt is happening and you'll soon be free to go. No big deal."

"Maybe not for you. How long will this take?"

"Hard to say. Could be quick, or it could take several hours. It depends."

"Several hours? I've got to call my husband." She remembered she didn't have her phone. "Can you get me to a phone?"

"Sorry, but it's against protocol. All we can do is wait. You're safe in here though."

Susan heard screaming and loud banging. "Are the prisoners throwing furniture against the wall? It sounds as if furniture is being tossed against the walls."

"No, ma'am."

Her neck was drenched in sweat and her chest felt tight. She sat on the floor, her back leaning against the wall. *Whatever made me think this was a good idea?*

Chapter 37

Lynette flew to her car, Annalise tucked under her arm. She floored the accelerator, almost hitting a tree on the way out of her neighborhood. On the way, she fumbled with her phone as she tried to call her husband.

"Jason, I'm on the way to the hospital. It's...it's my Dad. He was at work and...they said something about a heart attack. They couldn't reach my mom. Where the heck is she?"

"I'm on my way. I'll keep trying your mom. Don't worry. We don't know anything yet. He may be just fine."

Lynette's hands wouldn't stop shaking. She pulled into the first space she saw, and ran to the emergency room, Annalise clinging to her neck like a baby chimp. Out of breath, she pushed her way to the front of the triage line. "My dad, Mike Wiles. Where is he?" Her heart was pounding.

The nurse directed her through the doors, into the treatment area. She peeked behind several curtains, then addressed the first nurse she saw. "Mike Wiles. Heart attack. I'm his daughter. Where is he?"

"They took him upstairs for tests, then he's going to cardiac ICU. Take the elevator, turn right, and follow the blue line on the floor."

Lynette shifted Annalise to her other side, and ran to the elevator. She followed the nurse's instructions, and approached the cardiac ICU desk. "Mike Wiles. I'm his daughter. Is he here?"

"He's scheduled for an angiogram. We'll know more after that. Can you sign these forms for us? You *are* next of kin, right?" The nurse handed her a clipboard. "You can take a seat over there; put that pretty baby of yours down next to you."

Annalise had been crying ever since Lynette strapped her in the car seat. Lynette, usually patient, had heard enough. "Annalise, shut up! Stop crying."

Lynette clutched the clipboard. Her hand shook as she signed form after form. She couldn't believe they were making her fill out forms when all she wanted was to be with her dad. She had to know right now if he was okay. *Why did she have to do paperwork? Couldn't it wait till later?*

Without looking up, she said to the nurse, "My mother should be doing this, not me."

In a gentle voice, the nurse answered, "Your mother isn't here and we need consent. You want us to help your dad, right?"

Lynette grumbled. "You haven't seen my mom at all? Her name is Susan Wiles. She's short, pudgy, wears wire-rimmed glasses."

"No, honey. Other than you, the only other person who's been here was the man who brought him in. He stepped out to get a cup of coffee." The door swung open. "There he is now!" A tall, middle-aged man came up to her.

"You must be Mike's daughter. I'm Brad. I work with your father."

"Do you know what happened? He doesn't have heart problems. Are they sure it was a heart attack?"

"Yes. I stepped into your dad's office to go over some permit applications. He didn't look right. He was pale and sweating. I asked him if he was okay. He tried to answer, then clutched his arm—said it hurt. Then he said he couldn't breathe. I called 911 right away. Tried to reach your mother, but the phone went straight to voicemail."

"Did the paramedics say anything? No one's telling me anything."

"No. They slapped on an oxygen mask, hooked up some machine, gave him a shot of something. Then they loaded him into the ambulance and sped away."

Jason flew through the door just then and hugged Lynette close. "How is he? Did they tell you anything?"

Lynette relayed the information she'd gotten from Brad. "Did you reach my mom? She needs to be here."

"No, just keep getting voicemail."

Lynette whipped out her phone. "I'll call Audrey." She couldn't get service, and slammed the phone down on the plastic seat. "Forget it. I'm not going outside now." She fought back tears.

"Can I do anything more for you?" said Brad.

"No, go home."

Jason said, "Thank you for helping Mike." The man departed quietly.

Lynette paced, while Jason held Annalise. "Did you try Audrey on your?"

"Straight to voicemail."

"This is ridiculous. Neither my mom nor my grandmother is here. I'm not leaving until I know Dad's all right. It may be all night."

"I'm right here." He hugged her tightly.

The nurse offered Lynette a cup of coffee. "He's in good hands. Dr. Miller is the best cardiac surgeon around and he happened to be on call today."

"Surgeon? Will my Dad need surgery?" She felt her chest tighten like a vice.

"The doctor will talk to you as soon as he can. I know it's easy to say, but try not to worry." She pointed to the door. "Is that your mother now?"

Lynette shook her head. "Audrey! Where have you been? We tried to call. Is Mom with you?"

"No, I haven't seen your mom all day. Weren't the two of you supposed to go to the prison this afternoon?"

"Annalise is sick. I canceled the visit. How did you know we were here?"

"I got your messages. How's he doing?"

"They're still running tests. I don't know what's taking so long. I haven't been able to see him. I can't get in touch with my Mom. I figured she was with you."

Jason came back carrying two Styrofoam coffee cups. "Audrey! Is Susan with you?"

"No. I spent the afternoon antiquing. I haven't seen her."

Jason said, "Audrey, can you take Annalise to Susan's? We'll call when we know something."

"Of course." Audrey left with the baby.

"What's taking so long? It's been hours." Lynette's face sagged with fatigue. She kept a good poker face almost always, but tonight, she wore her concern like a neon sign over a Vegas hotel.

Jason said, "Let's think about this. Where could your mom be? Did she say anything earlier?"

"I told you I don't know where she is. I've been trying to reach her ever since I found out Dad was here. She wasn't with Audrey. We were supposed to go to Bayersville State this afternoon but….Oh, no! I bet I know exactly where she is!"

Chapter 38

Susan wiped her sweaty hair off of her face. Her stomach growled and her head was pounding. She pleaded with the guard, "Can't you get us out of here?"

"No, I told you, the prison has its protocol. They gotta do what they gotta do."

Susan paced around the confined area. She carefully bent her creaky knees, braced herself with one hand, and with the speed of a tortoise, worked her way to the floor, where she took a seat against the cinderblock wall. This wasn't how she'd planned to spend the afternoon. She fidgeted, trying to get comfortable.

"Do you have anything to eat on you?" asked Susan.

The guard pulled out his empty pockets. "Do I look like a vending machine?"

The lights flickered off. Panicked, Susan jumped up, threw her arms around the guard, and screamed, "What's happening? Are the prisoners taking over? We're going to die, aren't we?" She prayed out loud. "Hail Mary Full of Grace…"

The guard pushed her away, none too gently. "Will you stop your whining!"

A tidal wave of fear flooded her body. "What if I never see Mike again? I feel like I'll never see him again." The lights flicked back on. Susan's shoulders relaxed.

The guard folded his arms over his chest. "You're just making things worse. This kind of thing happens here almost weekly. It *is* a prison, you know."

"I have a daughter and a son. And a beautiful granddaughter. My granddaughter will never remember me. She'll tell all the important people in her life how her grandmother died in prison!"

"Knock it off. My ears need a break. Stop babbling."

Susan remembered how one time she'd stood outside the ladies room for ages thinking someone was in there. When she tried the rest room door again, it was unlocked. Excited at the new possibility, Susan pulled the door again. Darn it.

"What are you doing?" said the guard. "Do you think we'd be sitting here if the door wasn't locked?"

Maybe I should leave a goodbye note, just in case. "Hey, do you happen to have a pen and…" The guard put his finger to his lip. "Quiet," he demanded from behind clenched teeth. She checked her pockets. No pen. *Maybe I can scratch a note into the wall. I've seen that done in prison movies.* She had nothing to scratch a note with. She tried using her fingernail, but all she got out of it was a broken nail. The lights flickered off again.

Susan hugged herself. It was pitch black and her whole body trembled. "Do you think…?" She couldn't see the guard's face, but an unmistakable *shut up* pierced through the blackness.

Even if she came out of this alive, Lynette was going to kill her. *Why didn't I listen to her? I should have waited and rescheduled for a time we could both come.* She felt choked by the stale air. "I think the air conditioning went off too this time. Are you hot?"

"Lady, I'm hot and bothered is what I am. I said *shut up!*"

"Did you hear that? The alarm stopped. Maybe the prisoners disarmed it."

In a flash, the lights came back on, and Susan heard the door automatically unlock. The guard said, "Thank the Lord! Let's go. It's over."

Susan took a deep breath and race-walked through the remaining security station. Her body didn't relax until she was safely locked in her Prius. She'd have to drive back down the mountain road in the dark. She took her phone out of her purse to check the time, then noticed a dozen or so voice messages. She clicked on one and heard the words *Mike, hospital, and heart attack.* She thought she was terrified being locked in the prison, but nothing compared to the terror she felt now.

Chapter 39

Susan's heart pounded as she tore out of the prison parking lot. Lynette wasn't picking up her phone. Neither were Audrey and Jason. *I'm sure they're all together at the hospital. I can't believe I was locked in a prison while my poor husband was having a heart attack. What if he dies? What if he's already dead?* She had to calm herself down before she crashed and wound up in a hospital too. The drizzle from earlier in the day became a torrential downpour just as she turned onto the Thruway. Even with the wipers on the highest speed, she could barely see the road. *Come on, come on! Just my luck to get stuck behind a tractor trailer in the middle of a downpour when all I can think of is getting to the hospital.*

Thankfully, the truck didn't take the Westbrook exit. With the slippery roads and steamed up windshield working against her, she pushed the speed limit, pulled into the hospital parking lot, and flew through the rain into the emergency room.

"Where's my husband? Mike Wiles? He had a heart attack."

The nurse directed her to the cardiac ICU, where she found Lynette, Jason, and Evan.

"Mom, we've been trying to reach you all day. How could you disappear like that when Dad needs you here? He could have died."

"What's happening? Where is he? Can I see him?"

"He's having an angiogram. We're lucky we didn't lose him. We still don't know if he's going to pull through."

"I...I was at the prison..."

"Yeah, I figured that out after searching for you all day long. How dare you put me through that? I had to deal with the consent forms and the waiting. You should have been here with us."

"We were locked down. I didn't have my phone..."

"Save it." Lynette turned her back on Susan.

Evan gave his mother a hug. "She's upset like we all are. You're here now."

"Evan, what's going to happen? You had a rotation in cardiac. Is he going to die?"

"It's a good sign that he's strong enough to undergo the angiogram. The doctor should be out to talk to us any time now." Evan sounded brave, but Susan could tell by the tension in his jaw and the look in his eyes that he was as worried as the rest of them.

Lynette paced the floor. Jason put his arm around her. "Come, sit down. You must be exhausted."

The doctor came through the door at that moment, a serious expression on his face. "Come, sit down. We have to talk."

"Oh, my God! Is he alive? Tell me he's alive."

"Yes, Mrs. Wiles. He's out of the woods for now. We found a blockage, which is treatable. He has to avoid stress and be diligent about his lifestyle. Clean eating, exercise, meditation. It's a matter of life and death. You'll have to make sure he takes care of himself."

"Oh, I will. I really will. Thank you, Doctor."

Susan hugged Lynette's stiff body. "Thank God. Thank God he came through this."

Evan said, "He'll be okay. But you have to take care of him, Mom. Are you two still walking?"

"It's been too hot, but we will. No more excuses."
The nurse asked if they'd like to see Mike.

"Yes, of course," said Susan.

"Rules are only two at a time, but the unit isn't crowded tonight. Just keep it down. He's still groggy and weak. No stress. Follow me."

Bleeping machines and flashing monitors surrounded Mike's bed. Susan navigated the tangle of wires to give him a kiss. He opened his eyes, much to everyone's relief.

"Susan, you're here. Lynette? Evan?"

"Jason, too," said Lynette.

"Why am I here? Why am I so exhausted? I feel like an elephant is sitting on my chest."

Lynette explained the events of the day. Evan reassured him that he would be fine.

"How long do I have to be here?"

"Hush," said Susan. "We'll worry about that in the morning. You need to rest and work on recuperating." Mike's eyes closed.

"Mom, let's go home and let him sleep. We can come back first thing in the morning."

"We'll get through this together. Family is what it's all about," said Evan.

Susan knew family was at the top of her list, and made herself a promise. Keeping Mike safe and healthy was her new mission in life, ahead of volunteering, ahead of solving crimes. She felt a pang of guilt that it took a crisis to remind herself of her priorities.

Chapter 40

While Susan flipped through the heart-healthy recipe booklet from the hospital, Audrey creamed butter, milk, and cheddar cheese together in a glass bowl. There were only so many ways to prepare a chicken breast. Yesterday she'd baked it, today she'd go back to broiling. She stole a heaping spoonful of cheese sauce, and a handful of cooked elbow macaroni from Audrey. She finished whipping the potatoes, and carried them to the table.

"Mike! What are you doing? Put that salt down right now."

"Stop screaming like a banshee. I can't take any more broiled chicken and plain steamed vegetables. I want that." He pointed at Audrey's plate full of macaroni and cheese.

"I'm sorry; how insensitive of me. I can eat in the living room," said Audrey.

"Don't do that. It's just that your daughter is treating me like an invalid. I'm not asking for deep frying, or beer batter, but would a little seasoning on the chicken be so bad?"

Susan fumed inside. She was worried every hour of every day about keeping her husband alive. When he treated it as a joke, she wanted to smack him. She was afraid to leave the house for more than a short time. What if he had another heart attack and she wasn't there? Again.

"Susan says you're thinking about taking early retirement," said Audrey.

"Thinking about it. Right now I need three naps to get through my day. Maybe I'll feel differently when I'm recovered."

Susan added, "Retirement is wonderful. Think of all the things we'll be able to do together. We'll be with each other 24/7. We can travel, take classes..." She rubbed her hands together.

"Travel? With what money? With both of us living off a pension we'll be watching every penny."

Audrey said, "You can visit me whenever you'd like. It won't cost anything but the plane fare. Hey, you could spend your winters down in Florida with me. Be one of those snowbirds we all hate"

"I don't think Ludwig and Johann would appreciate being uprooted. And then there's your Wolfie. They've never been around a dog before."

"Did you hear a knock?" said Mike.

Lynette came through the door carrying a basket of fruit. "Jackson and Theresa sent this. Theresa says fresh fruit will get you back on your feet in no time."

"This is the second basket of fruit they've sent over this week. Overkill, don't you think?" He looked at Susan's disapproving face. "I'll call and thank them."

Lynette brought the basket into the kitchen, Audrey following behind.

"Lynette, now that your father is getting back on his feet, have you looked any further into Richard's case?"

"I haven't forgotten. When I can make the time, I'll go check out the evidence box myself. Maybe the missing glove is in there and they forgot to catalog it. Meanwhile, my priority is solving Shelley's murder case."

"Lynette, Dad and I were going to take our evening walk. Want to join us? How about you, Audrey?"

Lynette said, "Is he supposed to be doing that already?"

"The doctor said to start with short walks, just down the road and back."

"I'm too tired. Besides, *Jeopardy* is about to start," Mike whined like a toddler.

"On that note, I'm going home." Lynette gave her Dad a kiss on the cheek. "Love you."

Susan, Audrey, and Mike settled down in the living room in front of the TV. Susan was worried about Mike's mental attitude. Didn't he want to get better? The harder she tried, the more he resisted eating right and exercising. She wasn't about to stop pushing. *There's no way I'm going to be a widow at 63.*

Chapter 41

Lynette carried a steaming cup of coffee with her into work. She'd been up half the night with Annalise. Jackson was parked in front of the computer, eating a bagel stuffed with two inches of cream cheese. She shook her head at him.

"I know, I know. I brought a salad for lunch."

"Find any connections between Dakota Hall and hired hit men?"

"Nothing. Dakota has had exactly one visitor in the past year—your Mom. The guards say he doesn't talk to any of the other inmates, stays to himself, and keeps out of trouble."

Lynette leafed through Hall's file. "He's been a model prisoner. Makes a few dollars a week working in the prison laundry. No bank deposits, no phone calls…"

"I say he's clear. There's absolutely nothing that points at him arranging Shelley's murder."

"And my Mom said he looked genuinely surprised when she told him Shelley was dead."

"One more crossed off the list. That still leaves Clark Thibold, and Eddie, the custodian."

Lynette said, "Speak of the devil. Look! There's Eddie now, coming through the doors of our station all on his own." She stood up. "Good morning, Eddie. What can we do for you? You know we've been searching for you, especially since you locked my Mom in the school basement."

"I needed time, that's all. I had to clear my name."

"And you think you've done that?"

"Have a seat," said Jackson.

"I told you I loved Shelley. I even bought this for her." He pulled a black velvet box out of his pocket and opened it to show a small but pretty princess-cut engagement ring. "We were going to get married. I was planning to give this to her."

"How do we know you didn't hop over to the jewelry store and pick this up on your way here?" said Jackson.

"I have the receipt. Look. It's dated a week before Shelley died." He handed it to Jackson. "I also have our joint bank account information. As you can see, it's in both our names. I didn't have to kill Shelley to get access to her money. Besides, if it was money I was after, I'd have waited until after we were married to kill her. The school benefits include a life insurance policy. As it stands now, I get nothing. Why should I? I'm not her husband, though I wanted to be, more than anything. I brought you a copy of the policy."

"Not waiting until you were married to receive her life insurance money? That's your defense?"

"What if I have a witness who can vouch for me the afternoon Shelley died?"

Lynette said, "A witness? If you had a witness, you would have told us that weeks ago."

"It's complicated. You wouldn't get it."

"Detective Green and I are pretty smart. Try us."

"I was at a Gamblers' Anonymous meeting, okay? Emphasis on the *anonymous* part. That's why I stayed outside during Shelley's poker games. It took some convincing, but if you keep his name out of the newspapers, I found someone who will come in and sign a statement saying I was there all afternoon."

Lynette took the information. "We'll give him a call. Meanwhile, wait here." She went into Jackson's office to make the call. The witness agreed to come by and give a statement.

"Jackson, he's telling the truth. Another name crossed off our suspect list."

"Yep, another name. And then there was one."

Chapter 42

Mike promised Susan he wouldn't have a heart attack during the few hours she went to volunteer at the preschool. Besides, Audrey was at the house; he wouldn't be alone. The support they'd received from family and friends was above and beyond what Susan could have imagined. Theresa called every day to check on Mike and to ask if Susan needed anything. Rachel sent over a week's worth of dinners the day Mike was released from the hospital, and Vanessa made Susan a list of local resources, including stress reduction workshops, and heart healthy cooking classes.

Katie was straightening up the toys in the lobby when Susan arrived at the preschool.

"Susan, are you doing okay? How's Mike?"

"He's still tired all the time, but he's getting his appetite back. Of course, now he's craving rib eye and fried onion rings. Constantly complains about eating oatmeal and broiled chicken breasts, but too bad. I'm not letting him go through that again."

"Good for you. Men can be so dumb sometimes. They'd be lost without us."

Marin stapled a flyer to the parent bulletin board. "The grand opening of the rainforest exhibit is Saturday. I hope you'll both be there."

"Annalise and I are looking forward to it," said Susan. "Evan's come up this weekend. He and Audrey will be there too."

Marin pulled out her wallet. "These are invitations to the reception Saturday evening. Come as my guests."

Susan admired Marin's buttery soft wallet. She'd be looking for a new one herself. "Is that a monogram?"

"Yes. It's outdated but I'm unwilling to part with it."

"Outdated? Oh, I see. The monogram is *MK*. From your pre-marriage days?"

"Sure was. It was a Christmas gift from my Dad. Means a lot to me now that he's gone."

The day progressed without incident. The kids were no worse for wear. Music class went along as if no poisoning, murders, or heart attacks had ever happened. *Nice to be a kid.* Susan was surprised to see Lynette at the school midmorning.

"Lynette. What are you doing here?"

"Came to talk to Marin. You said she mentioned seeing Clark Thibold here at the school the day Shelley was poisoned. He's are top suspect, but we don't have enough to arrest him."

"Marin's in the teachers' lounge."

Lynette found Marin nursing a cup of coffee. "Tough day?"

"Got a lot on my mind, that's all."

"Marin, Mom tells me you saw Clark Thibold in the director's office the day Shelley was poisoned. Can you verify that for me?"

"Yes. Your mom showed me his picture. I'm sure it was him. He went in carrying a gift bag, then left. I figured he was a delivery man from one of the stores in town."

"Was anyone else in the lobby? Could anyone else have seen him?"

"I don't think so. Classes were in session. I'd just stepped out to take an important phone call."

Lynette jotted down the information. "What time was that?"

"11:30—before lunch."

Lynette brought the information back to Jackson. "Marin Weatherly saw Clark Thibold in the director's office the day Shelley was murdered, right before lunch. Lines up with what my Mom said. Mom leaves at noon and saw the gift bag in the office. Vanessa, the director, says she left her office for a few minutes before lunch and when she returned, the bag was on the table. Let's call Thibold. See if he denies it or not."

Jackson put the phone on speaker and called Clark Thibold.

"It wasn't me!" Thibold said. "I was on my way back to Scranton long before that. That woman is lying. Who is she anyway? I don't get why she'd say she saw me when I guarantee you I wasn't there. You can check with the hotel. I checked out right after breakfast."

"We'll do that. Have a nice day."

"Have a nice day? A bit sarcastic, aren't we?" said Jackson. I'll call the hotel."

Chapter 43

"Mike, did you finish your oatmeal? Did you remember to take your pills?"

"Yes to both. I wish you'd stop hovering over me, Susan. Aren't you supposed to be at the zoo this afternoon?"

"Don't use that tone with me. I'm trying to help you. Yes, Evan and Audrey are coming along. Why don't you come? I don't want to leave you here alone."

"Stop, already. I'll be fine. The last thing I want to do is listen to a bunch of boring speeches and pet South American snakes. Besides, I'm looking forward to some peace and quiet."

"You could use the time to fill out those pension forms. I thought you were turning them in last week?"

"Yeah, yeah. Susan, about that..."

Evan and Audrey came in from the yard. "I pulled some of those weeds out from around the hot tub. Evan threw some fertilizer on the rose bushes."

"Thanks, Audrey. Are you ready to go?"

"Let me grab the sunscreen and I'm ready."

Evan said, "I need to change my shirt. Be right down."

Susan turned to Mike. "What is it you were saying? About the retirement forms?"

"Never mind. It can wait till later."

Parking at the crowded zoo was tough. Susan drove around for quite some time, then managed to park just as Lynette and Annalise arrived.

"Doesn't she look adorable? That's the sundress Audrey bought her, isn't it?" said Susan.

"One of many. This one even has a matching bonnet. Thanks, Audrey," said Lynette.

"It's my pleasure buying clothes for my great-granddaughter. I'm so grateful I'm getting the chance to know her, as well as you and Evan."

They wheeled the stroller through the front gate, which was decorated with colorful balloon bouquets and streamers. They followed a cobblestone path to the rainforest exhibit, which was housed in a new, gray building with a large mural of the rainforest painted on one side, and a camouflage pattern on the other three walls. A ribbon stretched across the doorway. Background noises of tropical bird sounds, rustling trees, and flowing water emanated from two loudspeakers on either side of the door.

"Now I know why they wanted the opening in the summer. With the humidity and jungle sounds, I feel like I'm walking along the banks of the Amazon," said Susan. She spotted Marin, dressed in a dark green shift, in the center of the crowd.

"I'm so glad you all came," said Marin. "My stomach is doing somersaults. Time to give my speech."

"Is Trevor here?" asked Susan.

"Over there. With his father. I wish he'd just leave Trevor alone and stay out of his life. It's confusing for him to have a dad in and out of his life at this age, but far be it for my ex to put his son's needs first. Excuse me, I have to get things started."

Marin welcomed everyone, then introduced the other board members and thanked the benefactors. She explained that all of the animals inside the exhibit were bred in the Amazon rainforest and that much research had gone into replicating their native habitat. Then she cut the ribbon, and the crowd filed into the exhibit.

"Look! Is that a piranha?" said Audrey.

"Looks like one," said Evan. "Here, it tells about it when you press the button here."

"Snakes. I hate snakes," said Susan.

"Come on, Mom. I don't want you prejudicing Annalise against snakes. They only attack when they feel threatened."

Annalise pointed to a colorful frog.

Evan said, "Now those are far more dangerous than any snake. The blue ones excrete a deadly toxin. You've heard of people dying from eating blowfish? These little blue dart frogs are ten times more dangerous."

After finishing the tour, they exited to a canopied area filled with buffet tables. Imported cheese, caviar, champagne...expense had not been spared. Jackson and Theresa were munching on Swedish meatballs.

"Did Annalise like the exhibit?" asked Theresa. "I can't wait to take our baby here."

"She loved it," said Lynette. Her phone buzzed. "It's the Scranton police. I need to take this."

Trevor spotted Susan, and dragged his father over to her. "Miss Susan!" said Trevor. He gave her a hug around the knees.

"Hello, I'm Sam Weatherly, Trevor's dad. He seems to really like you." Trevor's father was athletically built, with blond hair and a warm smile.

"I teach music at his school. He's a super little boy."

"He sure is. I miss him terribly. His mother does her best to keep us apart, nut case that she's become."

"Marin seems quite civil to me. She's even stepped in to help teach at the preschool."

"The Marin I married was helpful, kind, loving...but she just never got over her father's death. It destroyed her. I did my best to help her cope, but in the end she drove me away."

"I lost my Mom not too long ago. It's still difficult; I miss her so much. Children have to expect they'll outlive their parents. That's life."

"Yes, but Marin's father was the target of an unforgiveable crime. It cost him every cent he had. She watched him wither away, until he finally couldn't cope any longer and shot himself in the head. It was horrible."

"Poor Marin." After absorbing the horror of the suicide, Susan thought about how alone Marin must have felt. She glared at Marin's husband, wondering how he could abandon his troubled wife. Married couples stick together, through thick and thin. *It's a miracle Marin has her life together at all with what she went through. She's a caring mother and gives back to the community –this whole zoo exhibit was spearheaded by her.* Susan wanted to hate this man standing in front of her, but oddly enough, he seemed genuine, not like the monster Marin had described.

Lynette returned to the buffet area after finishing her phone call. She pulled Jackson aside.

"They checked on Clark's story about getting home before Shelley was murdered."

"And?"

"His alibi checks out. His neighbor saw him pull into his driveway early in the afternoon. He couldn't have been in the director's office at 11:30 the day Shelley was killed. He couldn't have left the gift bag. He was already an hour from home by that time."

"But Marin Weatherly swore she saw him at 11:30," said Jackson.

"Either she's mistaken or she lied to us."

Chapter 44

"I'm exhausted from touring the exhibit yesterday," said Susan. "I'm not used to being on my feet for so many hours at one time."

Audrey said, "I'm glad I found these sandals downtown. My feet feel great." She wiggled her toes. "Are you up to taking a trip to the Livingston police station? Lynette is a doll, arranging for us to see the evidence from Richard's case first hand."

"You certainly put enough pressure on her. You realize she's giving up her Sunday for this, right?"

"I know, but if we find something to clear Richard, it will be worth it."

Lynette honked the horn, and they were on their way. They drove for several hours, arriving just before noon. Cement buildings, letters missing from signs, boarded up businesses—Livingston was every bit as remote and depressing as Bayersville. The police station was easily half the size but twice as quiet as Westbrook's. Lynette led the way.

"We've been expecting you," said the gray-haired officer. His face was doughy, his voice light and friendly—only his wrinkled hands hinted at his age. He led them to a musty room with a long wooden table. He pulled a heavy duty cardboard box from the shelf. "Hope it helps."

Lynette said, "I'll put everything back exactly as I find it."

"I'm not worried."

"Do you have a place for these two to wait?"

"They can stay and help you." He smiled at Susan with his twinkly blue eyes crinkling at the corners.

Not one to enjoy sitting on the sidelines, Susan was delighted to be allowed in on the action. "Thank you, officer." She smiled back.

"Let's get started," said Lynette. She opened the lid. "Looks exactly like what we saw in the photo." Lynette held the evidence list in one hand, and carefully placed each object on the table.

When she'd finished, Audrey dug through the box again and said, "I still don't see a glove, do you?"

"Nope. And here's the trial transcript. Nothing about a witness seeing a van." Lynette added, "I'll bet the neighbor boy was too young to be considered credible, so he was never called to the stand. The defense attorney should have insisted."

Susan noticed the shelves full of boxes with Sharpie labeled dates. "Lynette, are all those boxes full of evidence?"

"Yes, and since the town isn't a mecca for crime, looks like they have the room to house boxes from," she ran her hands along the shelves, looking at dates, "from 60 years ago or so."

Audrey said, "What if the evidence got put into the wrong box? Does that ever happen?"

"I guess it's possible," said Lynette.

"Do you think that happened with the glove? Maybe it's here in the wrong box."

"That's a long shot, but since we're here, I'll ask the officer if we can look into evidence boxes from around the same time as Richard's trial."

Lynette returned after a few minutes, telling Audrey and Susan that they had permission. They searched box after dusty box, disappointed each time.

"We gave it a try; that's the best we can do. Let's head back," said Lynette.

"No, please," said Audrey. "Let's check the same date but different years. Here's a box from the year before Richard's trial."

They opened it up, but found no glove. "Just one more, then we can go," said Audrey.

Lynette grabbed another box and took out the contents. In a clear, sealed bag, was a bloody glove. Audrey jumped up and down.

"Hang on, we don't know anything yet. This glove very possibly was found at the crime scene with this other evidence."

"Check it against the evidence list for that case."

"Okay, okay," said Lynette. She carefully read off each item listed. No glove. "Mom, do you have the list from Richard's case? Check the number next to the glove." Lynette matched it to the bag she was holding. "Bingo. This is the glove that was missing from Richard's evidence box. It must have gotten misplaced."

"And there's a big blood stain on it. We can get DNA!" Audrey clapped her hands.

"Hold your horses!" said Lynette. "We probably can, but not overnight."

"Can we get him a new trial? Maybe even have him released now?" asked Audrey.

"He has to get a good lawyer to petition for an evidentiary hearing. The judge makes the decision as to whether or not there's enough new evidence to warrant another trial. It could take months, and there's no guarantee. I wish we could locate the witness who saw the green van. It would strengthen the case for getting a new trial, providing he remembers anything from so many years ago."

"Lynette, you're the best detective and granddaughter anyone could wish for!" said Audrey, throwing her arms around Lynette.

"Okay, okay. Ready to head back? I'm starving. I saw a diner on our way in. Audrey, you owe me lunch." replied Lynette.

Chapter 45

"Good morning. How'd it go yesterday?" said Jackson.

"We found the glove in the wrong evidence box."

"Really? What kind of bozos work at that station?"

"Cooperative bozos to say the least. Now Audrey thinks freeing Richard is a slam dunk. She doesn't get that even if he gets a new trial, it could take years. The guy could be dead by then, and not because of capital punishment. He's already in his seventies."

Jackson poured Lynette a cup of coffee. "Let's focus on the murder case at hand. Clark Thibold's alibi checked out. We have his neighbor verifying he saw Clark pull into his driveway at 1:30. He had to have left Westbrook before 11:30 on the day Marin Weatherly swore he was in the director's office. Why would Marin lie?"

"She could have seen someone who looked like Clark. Or Clark's neighbor could be mistaken."

"Clark admitted to being at the school and breaking the window. But he denies leaving the threatening note on Shelley's desk—the one cut from newspaper letters. It got me thinking. From where and when did the suspect cut those letters? Look at this." Jackson opened a folder.

"It's the note that was on Shelley's desk."

"I compared the cut out newspaper words to the headlines from the *Westbrook Journal* dated the day of, and the day before, the note was left. I also looked at the *Scranton Times*."

"And?"

"Couldn't find a match in either paper for either day. Then I got to thinking, the note could have been written days earlier. Look."

Lynette examined the paper. "These letters are a match," said Jackson. "They're taken right off the front page of the *Westbrook Journal*, four days *before* the note was left. Same size, same font."

"Clark wasn't in town that day. He didn't leave that note."

"Then who did?"

* * * * *

Susan poured cat food into the bowls and Ludwig nuzzled against her legs. She closed the blinds to block the rising streams of sunlight, then poured Mike's prescriptions into the plastic pill sorter. She heard Mike coming down the steps.

"Mike, take your baby aspirin. Here, your oatmeal is ready. After you finish breakfast, go take your walk. You should be doing 20 minutes a day this week. I'll be back at the usual time. You have an appointment with the cardiologist at 2:00. We'll eat lunch, then go."

"Susan, stop! I can't stand taking orders from you. I'm a grown man. I can take care of myself."

"I know you can. I'm worried about you, every waking minute. I don't know what I'd do if you weren't around anymore. Who'd I get to shovel the driveway in the winter if you died?"

"It's not funny. You're driving me crazy. I look forward to when you're at the school."

Susan felt a lump in her throat, and held back her tears. "Better get used to it. Find yourself some retirement activities if you need your space, but we'll be spending a lot of time together from now on."

"No, I'm planning on going back to work as soon as the doctor okays it. As a matter of fact, I'm going to talk to my cardiologist this afternoon and see if he'll sign off on it."

"What? We talked about this, Mike! You're taking early retirement as planned. I even booked a cruise for us in the fall. It's non-refundable."

"I never agreed to retirement. I only said I'd think about it. I've thought about it and decided against it. You're going to be late." Mike stomped back up the stairs.

Susan fumed the entire drive to school. *What nerve he has. After all I do for him? If he took care of himself, I wouldn't have to hover.* She put on her happy mask and went into the school.

The director hung up the phone, and called to Susan. "Good morning. Are you okay? You look upset?"

Susan wished her emotions weren't so transparent. "Men. I'm worried about Mike, Vanessa, and we had a fight this morning. I'll be fine." Susan grabbed a doughnut from the teacher's lounge and took a big bite. Marin was tucking her lunch into the fridge. "Yum, did you bring these doughnuts, Marin?"

"Yes, I wanted to show my appreciation to all of you for showing up and supporting me Saturday at the rainforest opening. It meant a lot to me."

"We enjoyed it. I met Trevor's father."

Marin sighed. "If it weren't for Trevor, I'd never see that man again. He can follow his evil intents straight into hell as far as I'm concerned. Too bad Trevor can't have the kind of dad I had. Charley Kensington knew what it meant to be a father."

Chapter 46

Susan ruminated over her fight with Mike all morning long. By the time she left school, she'd decided to make peace. Maybe she *had* gone a little off the deep end over his health. She was looking forward to him retiring. They'd be able to take trips during off season, they could pick up Annalise and spend leisurely days at the zoo or the children's museum.

But then what? Mike enjoyed bowling, but wouldn't be hanging out at the alley all afternoon when his friends were all at work. Like herself, he wouldn't be entering retirement with a bumper crop of hobbies in which he could immerse himself. *He'll die from boredom, just like I did—until I found my sleuthing hobby. Maybe we could form a partnership, like MacMillan and Wife.* She quickly dismissed the idea.

"Susan, is that you?" Mike called to her from the kitchen. "I'm making turkey sandwiches for us."

Susan was relieved to hear Mike's tone had lightened. "Thanks." She gave him a kiss. "I'm sorry about this morning. I just get so worried, that's all. I have to learn to stay out of it."

"And to trust me."

"Of course. And if you aren't ready for retirement, I'm disappointed, but I understand. When I stopped teaching, the transition was harder than I'd expected."

"I'm considering cutting back my hours, maybe working part time. We can still do the cruise—me and you wrapped in blankets, watching the fall foliage go by while we guzzle beer on the lido deck..."

"Beer? I was thinking a nice white wine and imported cheese."

They finished lunch, and headed to the cardiologist, who declared Mike to be healing right on schedule.

The cardiologist said, "As long as you feel up to it, you can return to work in two weeks, but take it easy. Start by going in for a few hours and build up gradually. You'll be fine. Keep up the good work." He looked directly at Susan. "Both of you."

Susan gave Mike an *I told you so* look as they left the office. "Let's stop by Shop Rite. I invited Lynette and Jason to stop by for dinner. Maybe we could…"

"Grill a steak?" Mike rubbed his hands together. "How about a nice rib eye?"

Susan gave him a playful swat. "I was thinking more like chicken, but we can compromise. Lean ground beef, baked potatoes, low-fat frozen yogurt for dessert?"

"It's a deal. But I'm grilling the burgers."

At home, Mike took a nap while Susan straightened up the house. She was surprised to hear from Evan, who'd just gone back to the city last night.

"Evan, is everything okay?"

"Yes, fine. I called because of something we saw on Saturday. Remember those little blue frogs in the rainforest exhibit?"

"Yes, what about them?"

"I got to thinking, in their native environment, those frogs secrete a deadly neurotoxin. The natives coated their darts with it. Didn't Marin Weatherly say they'd just arrived, straight from the Amazon?"

"She did. Why?"

"Dart frogs bred in captivity lose their ability to defend themselves with their poison. It has to do with their diet."

"I appreciate the science lesson, but where is this going?"

"The teacher who was killed at your school was poisoned. I heard Lynette say it was a neurotoxin but they hadn't been able to identify it."

"Evan, you're brilliant! You think someone who had access to the frogs harvested their poison and used it to kill Shelley?"

"It's a rare toxin, and if someone wasn't testing for it they'd never find it. Marin Weatherly told me she'd been a zoology major when I met her at the memorial service. She had access to both the frogs and the school."

"Oh my God, Evan! You're right. She even taught science. But why on earth would she have wanted Shelley dead?"

"That I can't help you with. You and Lynette work on it."

"Thanks, Evan. Love you."

Susan's head spun. *It sounds too far-fetched to be true. Death by dart frog poison? Marin had no reason to kill Shelley.* Susan went into the kitchen and started preparing dinner. While chopping the cucumbers for the salad, the answer smacked her right in the face. *I know who killed Shelley and I know why.*

Chapter 47

Come on, Lynette. Hurry up and get here. Susan paced in circles around the kitchen.

Audrey asked, "Do you want me to mix the dressing? Mike went outside to light the grill. Are you okay, Susan?"

"Yes, just anxious for Lynette to get here. I have something important to tell her."

Susan heard a knock, and ran to the door. "Lynette, I solved the case!"

Lynette crossed her arms over her chest. "Which case, Mom?"

"Shelley's murder. And the attack on Katie, too. Sit down. You too, Jason and Audrey."

"I'm listening. Go on, Miss Marple," instructed Lynette.

"Evan called. He remembered Marin said she had a zoology degree. He noticed the blue dart frogs in the rain forest exhibit…"

"The *what* kind of frogs?"

"Blue dart. Evan told me they secrete a neurotoxin that's undetectable unless you're specifically looking for it."

"Mom, are you saying you think Marin killed Shelley using poison frogs? What possible motive did she have?"

"Marin was upset over her father's death. She blames his suicide on someone who, in her own words, *financially ruined him.*"

"You think Shelley and Dakota Hall swindled Marin's father?"

"Yes, Lynette! Think about it! I heard Marin say Trevor's dad was nothing like Charley Kensington. Charles Kensington—he's the man Dakota was arrested for swindling!"

Audrey said, "What makes you think it was the same person? That's not that unusual of a name."

"I'm sure it is," replied Susan. "Marin had a monogrammed wallet with the initials *MK*. Marin Kensington. She said she'd had it since before she was married. It was a gift from her dad."

"Ahh," said Audrey. "Trevor's father called Marin a nut case, remember? He was a charming young man."

"I will admit that Jackson and I were beginning to wonder about Marin. I'll call the crime lab and have them run a test for dart frog poison. While I'm at it, I'll get Jackson over here."

The aroma of freshly grilled burgers wafted through the sliding glass doors.

Mike came in from the patio holding a plate. "Dinner's ready! Hey, did I miss something?"

Susan filled him in on the details.

"Marin had access to the school and to the poison. She must have slipped the nicotine into Katie's coffee, thinking it was Shelley's," said Susan.

Audrey said, "Why didn't she use nicotine again when she poisoned Shelley? Why use such an exotic poison?"

"I'm guessing that when she saw that the nicotine wasn't strong enough, she came up with the idea of the frog poison, thinking they'd never detect it. Maybe she hoped the police would call it natural causes."

"No," said Lynette. "She lied about seeing Clark Thibold in the director's office on the day Shelley was killed. I think she wanted to pin it on him."

Susan heard a knock. "It's Jackson."

"The burgers are getting cold," said Mike. "Can't we eat while we finish this discussion?" No one seemed to hear him. Lynette caught Jackson up on their discussion.

Jackson added, "The letters in the note were taken from the *Westbrook Journal.* The one about evil following her into hell. Marin could have made it and slipped it on Shelley's desk. I bet when she saw Clark throw the hammer through the window, she saw an opportunity to point a finger toward him."

"Clark said he saw a woman and her son at the school the night before, when he was looking for Shelley. So, she knew he was in town," said Lynette.

"Evil following her into hell! I heard Marin use that phrase just the other day," said Susan.

Lynette's phone rang. "It's the crime lab."

All eyes turned to her. "They rushed the lab results. It was a slow night."

"And?" said Jackson.

"The poison, similar to the one blow fish secrete, came from a native South American frog. We got her!" Lynette's phone rang again and she answered quickly. Her face turned red, and she grabbed her purse.

"Oh, no! We have a jumper on the Hudson Valley foot bridge. Let's go!"

Chapter 48

Susan followed Lynette and Jackson to the wooden bridge. A patrol car and fire rescue had already arrived.

"Mom, I told you not to follow us. Go home!"

"Look, Lynette! Isn't that Marin?" She pointed up at the bridge.

The fireman called up to Marin with his megaphone. "Don't worry, ma'am! We'll get you down. Stay calm!"

"Don't come near me!" yelled Marin back to him. "It's too late! Tell my son I love him and I'm sorry!" Marin took another step toward the edge of the bridge.

"Get the ladder set up stat!" said Lynette. Jackson was already at the end of the bridge and moved closer to Marin.

"Don't come another step!" said Marin. "There's nothing you can say to change my mind!"

Susan ran toward the bridge too. Lynette ran after her. "Mom, no!"

Susan was undeterred. Despite Marin's protests, Susan wiggled around the rescue workers and got closer than they or Jackson had been able to.

"Marin, it's me, Susan! Take my hand. You don't want to do this."

"There's no choice," cried Marin.

"I know how hard it is to lose a parent. You had to be crushed when you found out about your dad," Susan spoke softly to the bereaved woman.

"He never should have died. *She* drove him to it. She and her husband." Marin's voice was hard.

"Think about Trevor," said Susan, pleading. "You know how it feels to lose someone you love. Think of the pain he'll feel." Susan climbed up onto the railing, nearly losing her balance. The water below was black.

Lynette yelled to her. "Get down, Mom!"

Marin yelled back. "If you come any closer, I'll jump right now! Go away, Lynette!"

Susan tried to take Marin's hand. "Think of Trevor. All his life he'll feel he wasn't important enough for you to stay with him. He'll think it was his fault. Do you want to ruin his life?"

"If I don't, he'll know his mom is a murderer. He'll never forgive me. What have I done?"

"Grab my hand tight. The court will understand. You had every right to kill Shelley. She killed your father. She wasn't even in jail—she got to live her life free as a bird!"

"I know! Why wasn't she locked up for life?"

"She deserved to be punished for killing a sweet old man. The jury will be on *your* side. Come down with me."

"You understand, don't you, Susan? You see why I had to kill her?"

"I understand, and I'm sure when Trevor is old enough he will understand too. I'll be by your side the whole time."

"You'll explain to the police?"

"Yes. Now come with me. If you go home now, you'll be there when Trevor wakes up in the morning."

Susan led Marin off the bridge, where Lynette waited with handcuffs.

"Mom, this was really crossing the line. I can't believe you climbed up on that railing. What were you thinking?"

"I was thinking how it would feel to be a little boy learning his mother had jumped to her death. That's what I was thinking."

All night long, Susan tossed, turned, and mulled over the reality of Marin being the killer. Marin had lost her father in a horrible manner and Shelley had been responsible. *Did that justify killing Shelley? Of course not.* She thought about the grief Shelley's parents would have to live with for the remainder of their lives. Shelley was a liar, a swindler, and a con artist, but she didn't deliberately set out to kill Charles Kensington. Susan's phone rang.

"Lynette, what's going on? Is Marin okay?"

"Yes, we sent her straight to the psych ward. She confessed. I called Shelley's parents. They're still raw with the pain of losing their daughter, but I think knowing we caught her murderer gave them a sliver of peace."

"What happens now?"

"Marin will be evaluated at the hospital and eventually brought to trial. She's facing years under lock and key."

"What about Trevor?"

"Trevor's father had picked him up before Marin went to the bridge."

"Good. Um. . . now that that's resolved..."

"You want to know if we got back the DNA from the glove, right?"

"Since you brought it up..."

"Not yet, but the evidence was definitely mishandled, and we located the witness."

"You located the witness? The boy who saw the green van pulling out of the Stirlings' driveway?"

"Yes. Richard Stirling's lawyer will take it from here. In my opinion, he has a good shot at getting another trial. Of course, it's the judge's call."

Susan told Audrey the news.

"That's wonderful! I told Richard I'd pay for the best defense lawyer I can find. Let's go see him. I'm sure he'd like to thank you and Lynette for what you did."

"Audrey, I spoke to George. He tells me you've drained your accounts helping Richard."

"I can sell the house. I don't need a big place like that anymore. It's just me. I'll be fine in a one-bedroom apartment."

"No, Audrey. You can't do that. You've gone above and beyond for Richard. Besides, we don't know he's innocent. The evidence was mishandled—true, but he still may have killed his wife."

Audrey continued to argue in favor of Richard's innocence. Susan had no idea how to convince her to calm down and take stock of her finances. She planned on calling George as soon as Audrey left the room. Guilty or not, Susan had a bad feeling about Richard Stirling. *Maybe I'll make one more trip to the prison.* She trembled thinking about it, but hoped she could convince Richard to leave Audrey alone. Besides, there was one more thing she wanted to ask him.

As soon as the barbed wire fence came into view, Susan cringed. This time, she'd begged Lynette to take a ride with her, but Lynette was too busy closing out the case. She took a deep breath, said a quick prayer, and went inside, where she was greeted by her new friend, the prison guard.

"You again?" The guard put his hand to his face and shook his head. "Didn't the lockdown scare you away?"

"Come on, now. Surely you remember what a brave woman I was in the face of danger. I have unfinished business here."

"As far as I'm concerned, I hope it gets finished today. Let's go." He led her to the visitation room, where Richard Stirling, in his orange jumpsuit, sat waiting on the other side of the glass.

"Susan, I can't thank you enough for your help. Your daughter, too. Finally justice will be served."

Susan felt a cold shudder run up her spine. *Finally justice will be served? What movie did he steal that line from?* She gave herself a pep talk. *Okay, Susan. Get over it, and focus on why you came here. You can do this.*

"Richard, Audrey's financial well has run dry. If you care about her like she thinks you do, don't let her pay for your defense. She's talking about selling her house in Florida. She's retired. What will she do when she uses up all her resources?"

"I'm not asking her to do it. It was Audrey's idea. If she wants to help, I can't stop her." He winked at Susan.

Yuck! This man is a first class creep. "There are lawyers looking for big cases like yours, just for the publicity. Perhaps you can find one who'll represent you for free."

"*Que sera, sera.* It's out of my control."

Please, God. Let the judge decide against granting him a new trial. Why had she helped him in the first place? She had one more piece of business here.

"Richard, I have to ask this one more time." She swallowed hard. "Are you my father?"

"Your father? Heavens, no." He laughed. Susan wanted to reach through the glass and smack him. Richard stretched his words out like hot caramel. "But I know who is."

"Susan's heart froze. "Who? Who is he?"

"Someone close to my heart. Or let's say, he once was."

"Stop talking in riddles. Tell me." Her fists were clenched so tightly that her knuckles hurt.

"Your father and Audrey were high school sweethearts. Grew up together—like two peas in a pod. One summer, he went away to Europe without her. That's when Audrey and I got close. It wasn't a romantic thing. I never felt the sparks on my end, if you know what I mean. I can't say she didn't. I'm kind of hard to resist. Especially back then. Umm, umm. I was a Clark Gable look alike."

Susan grew more frustrated by the minute. "Just tell me who my father is."

"I'm getting to that."

"What's his name? Is he still alive?" *This sadist really enjoys toying with me.*

"We all grew up together outside of Atlanta—me, Audrey, and your father. When he came back home in the fall, he ditched Audrey. Good thing I was there to pick up the pieces. The bum went away to law school. Shacked up with a new girlfriend right away. Then the bomb hit. Audrey found out she was pregnant. Hated him for abandoning her. She never told him. I was the only person she confided in. Outside of her parents, no one in the world knew she was going to have a baby. Her parents sent her away. Tried to pretend it never happened."

"Is he still alive? Do you know where he lives?"

"Sure. He moved backed to Atlanta. Lives in the house we grew up in. Still practices law."

"*We* lived in? As in you and him?"

"Yep." Richard leaned back and cradled his head with his hands. "Your father's my little brother."

THE END

ABOUT THE AUTHOR

 Diane Weiner is a veteran public school teacher and mother of four children. She has enjoyed reading for as long as she can remember. She has fond memories of reading Nancy Drew and Mary Higgins Clark on snowy weekend afternoons in upstate New York and yearned to write books that would bring that kind of enjoyment to her readers. Being an animal lover, she is a vegetarian and shares her home with two adorable cats and a little white dog. In her free time, she enjoys running, attending community theater productions, and spending time with her family (especially going to the mall with her teenage daughter and getting Dairy Queen afterwards). *Murder Is Developmental* is the fifth book in her Susan Wiles Schoolhouse mystery series and she has plans for many more.